DOC SAVAGE'S AMAZING CREW

William Harper Littlejohn, the bespectacled scientist who was the world's greatest living expert on geology and archaeology.

Colonel John Renwick, "Renny," his favorite sport was pounding his massive fists through heavy, paneled doors.

Lieutenant Colonel Andrew Blodgett Mayfair, "Monk," only a few inches over five feet tall, and yet over 260 pounds. His brutish exterior concealed the mind of a great scientist.

Major Thomas J. Roberts, "Long Tom," was the physical weakling of the crowd, but a genius at electricity.

Brigadier General Theodore Marley Brooks, slender and waspy, he was never without his ominous, black sword cane.

WITH THEIR LEADER, THEY WOULD GO ANYWHERE, FIGHT ANYONE, DARE EVERYTHING—SEEKING EXCITEMENT AND PERILOUS ADVENTURE!

Bantam Books by Kenneth Robeson
Ask your bookseller for the books you have missed

THE RED SKULL

A DOC SAVAGE ADVENTURE

BY KENNETH ROBESON

THE RED SKULL

A Bantam Book / published by arrangement with
The Condé Nast Publications Inc.

PRINTING HISTORY

Originally published in DOC SAVAGE MAGAZINE *August 1933*

Bantam edition / May 1967

2nd printing ...... *July 1967*	4th printing .... *October 1968*
3rd printing .... *January 1968*	5th printing ..... *August 1977*

ISBN 0–553–11319–4

Published simultaneously in the United States and Canada

Bantam Books are published by Bantam Books, Inc. Its trade-
mark, consisting of the words "Bantam Books" and the por-
trayal of a bantam, is registered in the United States Patent
Office and in other countries. Marca Registrada. Bantam
Books, Inc., 666 Fifth Avenue, New York, New York 10019.

Chapter I

THE HUNTED MAN

FIVE men were running across the golf links of the Widebrook Country Club. They kept in a compact group, and their manner was determined and sinister. Each carried a hooded golf bag.

The hour was near midnight. The moon sprayed a silver glow over fairways, sand traps and putting greens.

The five men drew no clubs from their covered bags. No golf balls lay on the fairways, not even luminous balls of the type sometimes used by those eccentric persons who play night golf. They were not indulging in a moonlight game—at least, not a golf game.

The five did not look like men who would turn to golf for recreation. They had calloused hands, thick necks and faces which were rocky and cold. Their skins were brown, leatherlike; their eyes had a habitual squint—marks of lives spent in a land of blistering heat and white-hot sunlight.

An observer would have wondered why they carried the shrouded golf bags, and would have been alarmed at their grim manner. But there were no observers. The Widebrook was one of the élite links in the vicinity of New York. Through the day, many persons of wealth played there. At night, there was only the watchman.

The watchman now lay in one of the clubhouse lockers. He was bound with rope ordinarily used to stretch the nets on the club tennis courts, and gagged with a sponge from the shower baths, held between his jaws by his own necktie. Moreover, he was still unconscious from a head blow delivered from behind. He had not seen his assailants.

"Get a move on, you hombres!" rapped the leader of the five runners. "We ain't got all night!"

This man had two scars, one on either cheek. They looked like gray buttons sewed to his leathery brown features, and indicated that he had been shot through the face sometime in the past. He was more burly than the others—his weight fell but a little short of two hundred pounds. He carried his bulk with the lightness of an athlete.

THE group sprinted on in silence, hugging the golf bags

1

to keep the contents from rattling. Then, at a command from the leader, they stopped.

"This is gonna be the place," he uttered as he waved an arm to indicate the spot.

"Are you certain about that, Buttons?" asked one of the others.

"Dang tootin'!" The wolfish smile of the man called "Buttons," made the scars on his cheeks crawl back toward his ears. "Whitey's telegram said it would be the No. 6 hole on this golf course. Whitey used to hang out around New York, and he knew about this place."

In a puzzled fashion, the first man peered around. "I don't see no number."

"You ain't lookin' in the right place! Blazes! Ain't you ever played golf?"

"Naw—and you ain't either! Why any grown man would fiddle away his time on this cow pasture pool is more'n I can savvy."

"Dry up. This is the sixth hole. The number was on that white box of a contraption back there. You crawl in that sand trap."

"You mean that hole full of sand? Do they call that a sand trap?"

"Hop into it!" snapped Buttons.

The other obeyed. With his hands, he hurriedly scooped a trench large enough to receive his form. Then he plucked open the hood on his golf bag, and drew from it a short, well-worn .30-30 carbine, as well as a single-action .45-caliber six-gun.

Shoving the six-shooter inside his shirt, the man stretched face-up in the trench he had dug. He placed the rifle on his chest, throwing his coat over the breech mechanism to protect it from the sand.

Buttons now plucked a large sheet of pale-brown wrapping paper from a pocket. He wrenched off a fragment, tore eyeholes in it, and spread it over the face of the man in the sand. Then he proceeded to cover the fellow with sand, leaving the paper-masked head in the open. The job completed, he stepped back for an inspection. He was satisfied. The pale-brown paper blended nicely with the sand.

"Swell! Anybody would walk right over you and not know you was there. You savvy what you're to do?"

"Yeah!" grunted the man in the sand. "I'm to pop out of here with my leadslingers, and get Bandy Stevens."

"But no shootin' unless we have to! Paste that in your bonnet. We gotta stop Bandy. Whitey's telegram said Bandy was wearin' somethin' bulky in a money belt around his waist, and we want to get whatever that is. But we wanta grab Bandy alive, so we can ask 'im some questions."

"Bandy Stevens is poison bad medicine! Don't forget that!" spoke the man through his paper mask. "Moreover, he is gonna be expectin' trouble, since Whitey tried to shoot him in Phoenix and missed."

"He don't suspect Whitey of that, the telegram said."

"Anyway, Bandy is poison——"

"A jasper named Buttons ain't no milk tonic, himself!" leered Buttons. "C'mon, you rannies! We'd better get set."

On the opposite side of the fairway, another man was soon planted in a sand trap. Two more were concealed in like fashion along the sixth hole of the golf course. Each man produced weapons from his golf bag.

Buttons, after hiding all his fellows, carried the empty golf bags to a convenient tree and hung them among the branches. Then he took refuge in the foliage beside them.

Silence now enwrapped the links. In the distance, automobiles moaned on a turnpike. A night breeze shuffled the leaves of the tree which held Buttons. A furtive, hopping cottontail rabbit came out and browsed on the grass of a putting green.

The waiting men were well concealed, and they maintained the patience of savage animals in wait for prey. There was no nervousness, no stirring about. However, each strained his ears to catch a sound for which they waited.

Buttons was first to hear it. A metallic mosquito drone in the distance! The noise grew louder and louder, becoming a throbbing howl.

Downward in the moonlight spun a plane. It was a two-place biplane, painted yellow, a little shabby. The big radial motor boomed gently as the craft floated over the links.

The two occupants peered earthward. The pilot was a tall, stringy man, hard of face. One thing distinguished his features—his eyebrows and small mustache were white as cotton.

The passenger, seated in the forward cockpit, was stocky. His skin, browned by hot suns, had also been reddened, where his helmet did not protect it, by the smashing wash of the propeller. His eyes were bleak behind the goggle glass; a huge jaw strained at his helmet chin strap. He was extremely bow-legged.

"Whitey!" he yelled at the pilot. "Are you sure there's room enough down there to land this sky bronc?"

"Plenty of room, Bandy. I told you I used to barnstorm around New York. I set my crate down on that golf course one time when my engine conked." The pilot with the white eyebrows and mustache leveled the plane, preparatory for a landing.

"Take another circle!" shouted "Bandy." "I wanta look the layout over some more. Since that shot at me in Phoenix, I figure somebody don't want me to get to New York. That's why we ain't landin' at a regular airport."

He dropped both hands into the cockpit and withdrew them, gripping a pair of businesslike blue six-guns.

At sight of the weapons, Whitey could not suppress a qualm. When he had hidden behind a hangar of the Phoenix airport where they had halted for fuel and food, and taken a futile shot at Bandy, it was nothing but luck that he had escaped discovery. He wondered if Bandy suspected the truth.

But Bandy was hanging over the cockpit rim, interested only in the ground. The plane cast a fleeing, batlike moon shadow.

The cottontail rabbit fled in terror from the putting green where it had been browsing. Bunny fashion, it popped into the handiest depression, which happened to be a sand trap which held one of the hiding men. There, the little animal caught the man scent. Association of the odor with shotguns and dogs brought greater terror, and the rabbit sailed back out of the sand trap the way it had come.

Bandy saw the incident, largely because the rabbit was a flashing gray spot against the luxuriant green of the fairway.

SUSPICIOUS, Bandy scowled at the sand trap. He knew the ways of wild things, knew how they reacted to danger. It was plain that something in the sand pit had frightened the cottontail.

"Fly close to them there sand holes, comin' back!" he bellowed over the motor thunder.

The pilot obeyed. He was unaware his aides were hidden there. He had merely wired them that he would land Bandy on the sixth hole of this golf course, a procedure suggested by Bandy's desire to avoid the commercial airports.

Bandy slanted one of his sixes at the sand pit. It tongued flame twice.

Neither bullet hit the man concealed below. But the fellow thought he had been discovered. Leaping erect, he drove a rifle slug up at Bandy.

The lead spanked through both wings of the plane.

"Yi-i-p, Powder River!" Bandy bawled the cowboy yell delightedly. He was elated that he had discovered the trap in time. Stretching far over the pit rim, he fanned lead at the rifleman.

In the rear cockpit, the pilot snarled and gave the controls a convulsive movement. The plane rolled over—in a flash, it was flying upside down. The object of the maneuver was to throw Bandy overboard.

Dropping both his guns, Bandy grabbed madly at the pit rim. His tough fingers gripped successfully. He kept himself aboard. But his weapons were lost.

Both cockpits of the plane held parachutes. Bandy had been using his for a cushion. It fell out, and the bow-legged little man dared not loosen his clutch long enough to seize it.

With an effort that made his arms ache, Bandy drew himself upward into the inverted pit until he could grasp the safety belt. Hanging to that, he twisted to face the pilot.

The flyer's face was desperate. It had faded until it almost matched the white of his mustache and eyebrows. He was wishing mightily that he had his gun—he had hidden the weapon after firing the shot in Phoenix, fearing Bandy might see it on him and become suspicious.

The plane was sagging earthward—but the pilot seemed not to notice.

"Hey—we're gonna crash!" shrieked Bandy.

The pilot saw their danger. He fought the controls. With only a few feet to spare, the plane rolled level.

Bandy leaned back and shook a horny fist under the airman's nose. "So you're in with them sand lizards down there! I'll bet you're the hombre who took that shot at me in Phoenix!"

A vicious glare was the flyer's reply. He was getting his nerve back, for it had dawned on him that Bandy was now unarmed. Moreover, the lost parachute gave him an idea.

RECOILING low in the pit, as though fearing violence, the pilot wriggled into the harness of his own 'chute. Then he sprang erect, leaned far back out of Bandy's reach, and stood poised for a leap.

"Climb out on a wing and stay there, or I'll jump!" he screamed.

Bandy hesitated, then he sagged back in the bucket seat. He knew when he was checkmated. He could not fly the ship.

"You win!" he gritted.

"Get out on the wing!" the pilot bellowed through the motor clamor.

Bandy obeyed. The dangerous performance of climbing out and hanging to a brace wire did not bother him much. Bandy had plenty of nerve.

He watched the flyer. The instant the fellow gave his attention to circling the plane back to the golf course, Bandy flicked his fingers inside his shirt and unbuckled the chamois money belt he wore. A single jerk would now remove the belt.

Bandy turned so that his back was to the pilot. From a coat pocket he dug an envelope and a stubby pencil. The rushing air threatened to tear the envelope to bits in his fingers. Holding it close to his chest, he managed to scrawl words:

$500 REWARD FOR DELIVERY OF
MONEY BELT TO DOC SAVAGE.

Bandy glanced slyly over his shoulder. The pilot apparently had not noticed; he was peering downward, engrossed in the ticklish business of making a moonlight landing.

Folding the envelope, Bandy stuffed it under a flap of one of the money belt pouches.

The motor noise lessened, becoming slow explosions which barely turned the prop over. Less than a hundred feet up, the plane floated down for the golf course.

A paved road, narrow and apparently not much used, bordered the links. Just before the ship passed over this, Bandy dropped his money belt. He flashed a look at the pilot, and heaved a relieved sigh. Bandy was in partial shadow between the wings, and his furtive movements seemed to have escaped detection.

The chamois belt fell a few feet from the road. Bandy bit his lower lip savagely. He had hoped it would land on the pavement. However, it reposed where it could be seen.

The note promising a five-hundred dollar reward should insure delivery of the belt to the individual Bandy wished to have it—Doc Savage.

Bandy scowled doubtfully. Suppose the finder of the belt should be unable to locate Doc Savage? But that was hardly probable.

Doc Savage—the man whose astounding reputation had penetrated even to the acrid waste land of Arizona—would be widely known here in New York.

Chapter II

THE DEATH TRICK

THE pilot fish-tailed the plane—a maneuver effected by treading the rudder—to decrease air speed. The ship grazed a putting green, then three-pointed wheels and tail skid in a perfect landing. Bouncing a little, the craft coasted along the fairway.

Bandy came to life. He was back on his element—the earth. Briefly, he considered jumping off the plane and taking his chances on a sprint for cover. He dismissed that idea as too risky. The riflemen would pick him off.

Balancing expertly, he leaped along the wing. A vaulting spring landed him atop Whitey in the control cockpit of the plane.

"Pull a fast one on me, huh!" hissed Bandy, and speared an accurate fist through the arms the pilot raised defensively.

The blow smacked loudly on the flyer's temple. The man gurgled. Agony made his eyes stick out. He grabbed his throat protectively with both hands.

Bandy belted him on the exposed jaw. The pilot began to tremble and make the aimless, feeble gestures of a man half knocked out.

A .30-30 slug plowed past Bandy's head with a sound akin to that of a breaking banjo string. The five ambushers were sprinting for the rolling plane, shooting as they came.

Lifting the dazed pilot bodily, Bandy threw him out of the ship. He knew which lever was the throttle. He knocked it wide open. The craft streaked forward.

More bullets lashed the plane. Bandy dived into the rear cockpit. It offered scant shelter. Lead gored the padded pit rim. A slug dug glass out of the instrument board and the fragments cut Bandy's leathery face.

The plane took a goatlike bound. Bandy hastily cut the throttle, not wishing to leave the earth. The ship had veered to one side in its wild charge. Bandy saw shadowy trees shoving up ahead and hastily covered his face with his arms.

There was a jarring crash. The ship spun. One wing had hit a tree. The craft nosed over, the prop digging up a cloud of grass and black earth. With a lazy crunching and a shrill tearing of doped fabric, the plane settled on its back.

Bandy was thrown out. He had not been harmed much. Bucking broncs had often given him worse shakings. He heaved up and ran.

Trees grew thickly in the copse in which he found himself, and lead began scuffing off bark and clattering fiendishly among the branches. The howling voices of his pursuers reached his ears.

"Run, you galoots! We can't let that hombre get away!"

Bandy hissed in astonishment as he recognized the voice. "Huh! That guy is Buttons Zortell! He was workin' on the job as a powder fitter until a couple of weeks ago!"

COLLISION with a tree silenced his rumination. He ran more carefully, striving for silence. But he was too bow-legged to be graceful on the ground. He jarred small bushes noisily. Twigs cracked underfoot.

Buttons and the other pursuers followed the sounds. They gained steadily.

A woven wire fence abruptly confronted Bandy. The top was armored with two strands of barbed wire. Going over, he scraped his hands on the barbs and left behind a fragment of his coat.

Ahead, across an open pasture, stood low sheds. He legged it for these. He made a hundred yards—a hundred and fifty. Then a bullet scraped through the grass underfoot. Gun sound lunged thunderously across the meadow and caromed in fainter gobbles from trees and buildings.

Bandy pitched alternately right and left as he ran, making himself a difficult target. He rounded the squat sheds.

About to go on with the buildings as shelter, he heard noisy stampings and blowings within the structures.

"Hosses!" he chortled, and dived inside.

The stable shed held several sleek animals. They were saddlers, long-legged, graceful.

Bandy flung to the halter of the nearest horse. A single wrench freed the knot. He mounted. Halters hung on a peg beside the door—four of them. Bandy grabbed all four as he rode out.

A few rods beyond was a stone fence. Bandy heeled the horse for the obstacle. The animal cleared it easily. Simultaneously, a fresh volley of rifle fire clapped out. Buttons and his men had rounded the sheds.

The pursuers did not stop for horses, but came on.

Bandy found himself riding across an oat field. The grain, yellowing with ripeness, reached almost to his dangling feet. Across the middle of the field ran a small gully. Trees were scattered along this gulch. Bullets tore the foliage of these.

Two score feet from the concealment of the trees, Bandy flung himself half off the horse, pretending to be hit. He guided the animal into cover. Then he worked swiftly.

With the four extra halters, he rigged a collar on the horse, with traces reaching back on either side. To the ends of the traces, he tied what was left of his coat, forming a drag. He seated himself on that and clucked at the animal. The saddler ran away across the oat field, hauling the man.

It was an old trick of the Indians that Bandy was employing. He held onto the drag and kept his head below the level of the oats.

Buttons Zortell caught sight of the running horse. In the

moonlight, he failed to discern the rude harness, or the man it pulled.

"We winged 'im!" Buttons yelled. "He fell off the cayuse! Look sharp, you hombres! He's probably layin' in that ditch somewhere!"

They began searching along the gully.

When a fence stopped the running horse, Bandy rolled off his improvised sled. Scratched and raw, he crept away. A wide circle took him to the narrow road, and to the spot where he had dropped his money belt. He retrieved the belt. Then he set off down the road, running easily.

"Now to get in touch with this Doc Savage gent," he told himself.

BUTTONS ZORTELL, unable to find a trace of his quarry, was cursing his men, himself, the moonlight and whatever else came to his mind.

The frightened horse, head up, loped about the oat field. Buttons suddenly discovered the halter ropes dragging behind the animal. He released a coyote-like howl of rage.

"The bow-legged runt pulled a fast one on us!"

"I told you he was a bad jasper to monkey with," muttered one of the men.

"We ain't licked yet! Let's see if we can locate 'im!"

They conducted an intensive search. The spot where Bandy had left the pad dragged by the horse, they found. But that was all.

"C'mon!" ordered Buttons. "I've got another plan. And we gotta get away from here. Somebody is sure to look into all that shootin'."

"What about my plane?" wailed the pilot. "It can be traced to me, on account of the identification numbers painted on it."

Buttons had no trouble solving that problem.

"We'll burn it!"

They found the wrecked plane already drenched by gasoline which had leaked from a tear in the fuel tank. A lighted match thrown from a safe distance caused it to become bundled in roaring flame.

The men ran to a car, which they had secreted near the clubhouse. Not until the machine was bearing them speedily toward New York, did one of the crew voice a question.

"What are we gonna do, Buttons?"

"Bandy is tryin' to get to a hombre named Doc Savage. We'll head 'im off."

"Blazes! How'd you find that out?"

The scar-cheeked leader leered knowingly. "The big boss

told me, before we left Arizona. Me and him listened through
the cracks in a log shanty while Bandy was gettin' his orders.
Bandy was sent east to ask help from Doc Savage, and he's
carryin' a letter and a bunch of papers in that money belt.
We gotta keep Bandy and his belt from gettin' to Savage."

"How?"

Buttons growled fiercely. "I'll show you!"

HEADLIGHT beams waved stiffly ahead of the fast-moving
car. Night insects looked like fluttering bits of white paper
embedded in the white glare. Tire treads sucked and whis-
tled on the pavement.

One of the men put a query. "Who's this Doc Savage?"

"I'll tell you the thing about 'im that hit me most,"
Buttons replied grimly. "The boss has never seen Doc Savage, yet he's scared stiff of the gent!"

"The boss—scared!" The questioner snorted unbeliev-
ingly. "With an organization like the boss has, he shouldn't
be leary of anybody."

"Well, he is! And he's droppin' everything else, so as to
give all his attention to keepin' Savage from gettin' mixed
up in this business."

Buttons, who was driving, wheeled the car around a
sharp curve before he continued speaking.

"I don't know as I blame the boss, at that. I got a newspaper on the phone as soon as we hit New York. They gave
me the dope on Savage. What I mean, it was plenty! I figured
at first they was kiddin' me. So I called another newspaper
—and they told me the same stuff."

Buttons glanced around and saw he had a very interested
audience. The men were leaning forward to catch his words.

"I'm still wonderin' if the newspapers was stringin' me,"
he continued. "No one man could be all they said Doc Savage was. Accordin' to them, this jasper is the greatest surgeon
in the world, as well as the greatest engineer, the greatest
chemist, the greatest electrical expert. Hell! To hear them tell
it, nobody can do anything better than he can! Now I ask
you gents—don't that sound like bushwa?"

The listeners blinked and exchanged doubtful glances.
They did not know what to think.

"I got Doc Savage's life history," Buttons snorted. "It
seems his dad trained 'im from the cradle to make a superman out of 'im. The old man's idea was to fit Doc for what
the newspaper gents called a 'goal in life.' I gathered that the
goal is to go around huntin' trouble and nosin' into other
people's business.

"If a hombre gets in a jam, he can go to Doc Savage, and

hocus-pocus, presto!—Doc fixes him up. Just as easy as that! And it don't make any difference if the guy in the jam ain't got no money to pay. Doc ain't a money proposition."

"Sounds nutty to me," muttered a man.

"Same here. But the jasper must amount to somethin', or he wouldn't have a rep like that. And, remember, he's got the big boss worried. I found out somethin' the boss didn't know."

"What's that?"

"Doc Savage has five hombres who work with 'im. They're specialists in certain lines. One is a chemist, one an engineer, one an electrical expert, another an archæologist, and the last one a lawyer. I learned their names, what they look like, and where they live. I got the same dope on the Savage feller."

"Knowin' all about 'em will help us."

"Sure, it will. We'll have to go up against the gang if Bandy Stevens gets to 'em. I got an old newspaper an' cut their pictures out of it."

BUTTONS waited until he was piloting the car down a straight stretch of road, then fished a news clipping from an inner pocket. He spread it for the others to inspect.

The clipping was a picture. It showed a group of six remarkable-looking men. They were attired in formal fashion, with top hats and claw-hammer coats.

Buttons put a finger on the most striking character in the assemblage. "This one is Doc Savage."

The other men stared closely. They were impressed, suddenly realizing this was no ordinary personage about whom they were talking. Even the vague printing of the newspaper cut did not diminish the aspect of strength and power about the giant form of Doc Savage.

"That hombre ain't nobody's pushover," muttered a man.

"Look at the gents with 'im!" grunted another. "One is darn near as big as Doc! And pipe the hairy gorilla of a feller! Imagine meetin' somethin' like that in a dark canyon!"

"The skinny one with the glasses don't look so bad. Neither does the shriveled little runt, or the one who wears his clothes so fancy."

"What does it say at the bottom of the picture?"

Bending close, they read the fine newsprint beneath the clipping:

Clark Savage, Jr., and his five associates at the ceremonial cornerstone-laying of the Savage Memorial Hospital in Mantilla, capital city of the Luzon Union.

"What was the story with this picture?" a man wanted to know.

Buttons hesitated, then answered reluctantly: "A yarn about this Doc Savage savin' the Pacific island republic, the Luzon Union, from a lot of pirates who had come down from the China coast and were tryin' to take over the government. Doc wouldn't take a reward, so they put up the hospital in his honor."

The men seemed somewhat stunned. They moved their hands nervously.

"Jumpin' steers!" said one uneasily. "The gent ain't a piker!"

Buttons Zortell sneered loudly. "Don't let a jasper's rep get your nannies! We ain't a bunch of slant-eyed ginks, like them pirates the paper told about. And glom onto this—the big boss ain't a slouch himself, when it comes to brains!"

Little more was said. The car had entered New York, and driving the unaccustomed streets required all of Buttons's attention. Due to the late hour, there was little traffic.

Locating Broadway, Buttons drove along that thoroughfare. A halt was made at a shabby hotel where he and his men had taken rooms.

Buttons entered the hostelry. He reappeared within a few minutes, carrying a metal-bound steamer trunk.

An opening in the end of the trunk was covered by a stout metal screen. Through this came scratchings and whimperings.

"What the blazes?" demanded one of the crew. "I been wonderin' why you brought that——"

"Wait and I'll tell you!" Buttons snapped. He stared about to make sure no one was near, then leaned over and spoke in a low voice: "The big boss knowed we might have to do some croakin'! So, before we left for the East, he gimme some sweet tools to do our work with!"

"Whatcha mean?"

Buttons leered at him knowingly. He dropped a hand on the steamer trunk from which the weird noises came. "This is one of the little things the boss gimme! What's in this trunk will salivate Bandy Stevens plenty! It'll do the job so there won't be a chance of us gettin' caught."

Entering the car, Buttons wheeled it downtown. He was heading for one of the tallest skyscrapers in the city—a towering structure, the eighty-sixth floor of which housed Doc Savage's headquarters.

Chapter III

FANGS

ONE thing distinguishes New York from other cities—the number and height of its office buildings. Gothamites can boast of their skyscrapers without fear of contradiction. And few of the cloud-piercers were the object of more bragging than the structure which housed Doc Savage's office, library, and experimental laboratory.

To a height of almost a hundred stories, the skyscraper reared. Outside, the architecture was severely plain, in the modernistic fashion. The few decorations were in a shiny metal which was impervious to the weather. Inside, the fittings were elaborate and costly. More than fifty passenger elevators served the tenants.

Bandy Stevens hung his head out of his taxi window and studied the imposing edifice with no little awe. Bandy had secured a lift from a passing motorist and ridden until he had encountered a cruising taxi. The cab had hurried him into the city.

No cars were parked near the great office building at this night hour. Only one man was to be seen—a shabby fellow who sat on the walk near the entrance of the building. This man maintained a hunched position, and wore dark glasses. He held a bundle of newspapers, which he seemed to be offering for sale. A small bulldog crouched at his side, head on its paws, as if dozing.

Bandy peered upward at the face of the skyscraper. A number of windows were lighted. He decided this merely meant the janitor force was at work.

He had scant hope of finding Doc Savage here at this time of night. But he hoped to locate some one who would tell him where Doc could be found. This address was the only one Bandy possessed.

The taxi drew to a halt before the tower of steel and masonry. The driver was not courteous enough to take the trouble of opening the door for his fare.

This driver was a surly individual. His neck was a thin stem, and his head perched atop it like a puckered fruit.

"Five dollars," he said, naming the fare.

The charge was too much, but Bandy did not argue. He dug out a roll of notes which made the taxi driver's eyes glitter greedily, and peeled off a bill. Bandy was peering about in search of danger, and failed to notice he was handing over a ten-spot. The driver pocketed the bill quickly, and made no move to give change.

The vender of newspapers, seated on the walk, kept his head down. He had one hand on the neck of his dog. There was nothing suspicious in his manner. He might have been asleep.

Bandy started for the skyscraper entrance.

The newspaper seller gave his dog a shove in Bandy's direction, and released the animal. The canine sped for the bow-legged man. Its jaws were distended, its fangs showing. There was something hideous, deadly in its charge.

Bandy strode ahead. It seemed certain he would be bitten before he dreamed of danger.

For the second time that night, Bandy's sharpness of eye saved him. In the highly polished metal of the modernistic door ahead, he discovered the reflection of the canine.

With a quick wrench, Bandy got the door open. He sprang into the air. The snapping teeth of the animal missed him. The smooth tiling underfoot afforded poor purchase for the beast's claws. It skidded through the door into the lobby, striving desperately to turn for a second attack. Bandy slammed the door, shutting the animal in the lobby.

He flung a look at the newspaper vender. The man was on his feet, fumbling inside his clothing as if after a gun.

It was Buttons Zortell!

Across the street, two of Buttons Zortell's henchmen popped out of a shadowy doorway.

Bandy was still unarmed. He thought quickly. Two routes of flight were open. Through the lobby meant facing the canine, and there was something strange and deadly about the creature. Bandy chose the second—the taxi. He hurled into the cab.

"Drag it away from here, fella!" he yelled.

The driver cursed. He had been on the point of going on, and had the gears in mesh. He let out the clutch. The machine sprang ahead.

The two men on the opposite side of the street lifted guns.

"Don't shoot!" bellowed Buttons Zortell. He wanted no gunplay downtown. He and his men, strangers in the city, would hardly be able to evade the police.

The taxi lunged past the first street intersection. Looking back, Bandy saw a car careen out of the side thoroughfare. Buttons Zortell and his men ran for this machine and piled in. Buttons had recovered his bulldog, and was carrying the beast under an arm.

"Step on it!" Bandy rasped at his driver. "They're gonna ride our tail!"

Over his shoulder, the driver snarled, "If yer runnin' from de law, don't t'ink I'm gonna——"

"They ain't the law! Twist the tail of this gasoline steer! Let 'er rip!"

The cab took a corner at the head of an arc of smoking tire tread and volleyed across town. It turned again, passing a policeman who promptly sprinted for the nearest call box.

Buttons Zortell's machine was hot on the trail, Bandy discovered.

"We'll have half de radio patrol cars in town after us if we keep dis up!" wailed Bandy's driver.

Bandy considered. He would have welcomed the police, but there was a good chance they would not overhaul him in time. The car behind was gaining—it was a more powerful machine.

"What's the busiest corner in town?" Bandy demanded.

"I dunno. Forty-second an' Broadway, maybe."

"That one will do! There's a hundred bucks in it for you if you'll meet me there in an hour! Will you?"

The driver negotiated another corner. "A hundred berries? Yeah, I'll meet you! For dat much jack, I'd meet Old Harry himself!"

Bandy hastily stripped off his money belt. He jammed it down back of the seat cushion, out of sight.

"Lemme out at the next corner," he commanded. "I can come nearer losin' 'em if I'm afoot."

The cab promptly squawled to a stop. Bandy whipped out. "Don't forget to meet me in an hour, partner!"

He made a mental note of the cab license, then sprinted around the corner. A dimly lighted hole yawned before him. Steps led down into this. It was a subway entrance— the first Bandy had ever seen.

He descended the steps with bow-legged jumps. A string of cars stood at the platform. The doors were all closed; the cars were beginning to move. Bandy vaulted the turnstiles, not bothering to find how one paid fare.

Most of the subway car windows were open. He dived at one—got inside. The train plunged into the tunnel like a bellowing monster.

Bandy grinned and wiped perspiration off his leathery features. "Huh! If I'd knowed it was gonna be this easy, I'd have kept that belt!"

He imagined he heard angry yells through the train noise —probably his pursuers cursing him from the station platform. He grinned more widely, imagining their discomfiture.

BACK in the subway station, Buttons Zortell had sent one loud, angry expletive after the receding train. He and his men had arrived possibly twenty seconds too late.

"He's gone—the homely little pill!" Buttons groaned. "Damn! I thought sure I had 'im when I sicked the bowser on 'im!"

Perceiving the man in the change booth eying them suspiciously, Buttons and his men hastily returned to the street. There, they held a disgusted council.

The bulldog leaped out of their car, which Whitey had been driving, and scampered up. The men recoiled from the beast as from a rattlesnake.

"Blazes—supposin' the pooch should bite one of us!" croaked a man.

Buttons carefully captured the animal, and from its front teeth removed a plate of sharp-pointed metal spikes. This was ingeniously made, each spike holding a small hypodermic needle. Had the dog bitten Bandy, the pressure of its jaws would have forced the contents of the needles into the wound.

"There's enough poison in here to drop a longhorn quicker'n you could snap a finger," Buttons grunted, gingerly stowing the grisly contrivance in a metal case and pocketing it. "The dog belongs to the boss. He's been trained to bite anybody he's set on."

"Nifty," admitted one of the group. "Only it didn't work this time."

THE taxi in which Bandy had arrived, still stood at the curb. The stringy-necked driver now leaned out to call, "Hey, youse guys!"

"Don't pay any attention to 'im!" snarled Buttons.

They started toward their own machine.

"Let's me an' youse boids have a talk!" suggested the taxi driver. "I t'ink maybe we can do each odder some good."

Buttons Zortell hesitated. "The tramp probably wants us to slip 'im a few shekels to keep 'is mouth shut! I'll throw a scare into 'im!"

Approaching the hack, Buttons snapped: "What d'you want, ranny?"

The cab driver studied the burly Westerner. "Was youse guys after somethin' de little punk was carryin'?"

"What if we was?" Buttons demanded belligerently.

"Aw-w, don't get hard about it! I just thought I might be able to help yer."

"You interest me strangely, pard," said Buttons in a tone

that was suddenly soft and purring. He recognized a kindred soul in this taxi pirate.

"What's it worth to youse to get de money de guy was wearin'?"

"Ten bucks," said Buttons cautiously.

"Blah! Whatcha take me for? I want five hundred!"

Buttons's gun hand made a move for his pocket. Then he reconsidered. After all, it was best to avoid violence here in the strange city. And it was not his own money he was spending. He could put it down on the expense account he would turn in to his sinister employer.

"All right," he grumbled, and produced a well-stuffed wallet.

The taxi driver counted the money over carefully. Then he drew Bandy's belt out of his shirt. He had seen his passenger conceal it, and had examined it, hoping to find money. There had been no currency, much to his disgust.

Buttons Zortell climbed into the cab to inspect the belt contents. Two envelopes came to light one large and brown, the other small and white. He rifled through the larger.

"This one is just maps and plans and stuff," he grunted.

The little white envelope held a letter. The scar-cheeked man read this through. Several times, he grimaced in a manner which showed great satisfaction.

"It's lucky we got this!" he told his fellows as they clustered about.

"I was to get a hundred berries for deliverin' dat to de little guy in an hour," whined the taximan. "Ain't dere some way for me to collect dat jack?"

Buttons began to grin. He crashed a palm upon his knee in delight.

"You've given me an idea, hombre!" he chortled. "Not only can you collect, but I'll pay you another hundred simoleons on top of that! All you gotta do is follow my orders!"

"O. K." The driver's sour face was avid with greed.

"We don't wanta take any chances on Bandy gettin' to Doc Savage," muttered a man.

"Don't worry," Buttons chuckled. "I've got a system for takin' care of Bandy. There won't be any more slips."

The taxi driver stared at Buttons. Uneasiness had replaced greed on his dour features.

"Did I hear yer say somethin' about Doc Savage?" he questioned.

"Yeah."

"Den count me out of dis!"

"Hell!" snarled Buttons. "What's eatin' you?"

The hackey shivered. "I ain't gettin' near dat bronze guy."

"Bronze guy?"

"Ain't yer ever seen Doc Savage?" The driver was incredulous. "He looks like a livin' statue made outa bronze metal. I wouldn't go up against dat guy fer no man's money. A pal of mine tried to croak 'im once—an' dropped outa sight! I didn't see de pal for months. Then, a couple of weeks ago, I ran onto him.

"It was awful! Doc Savage had done somethin' strange to de poor feller. He didn't even recognize me, his old pal! He didn't know his own father, who is a big shot on de East Side. I tell yer, it gimme de jitters to watch 'im!

"An' when I told 'im where he could get a job peddlin' dope, he hauled off an' knocked me down, den walked away. I'm tellin' yer—Doc Savage ain't human. He worked some kind of black magic on my buddy. I don't want no part of 'im!"

Buttons Zortell snarled angrily. He could see this weird tale had had a distressing effect upon his men. He did not want their courage undermined by such talk.

"We're not scared of this Doc Savage!" he snapped.

"Dat's what my pal said," retorted the driver.

"Hell an' damnation!" Buttons roared. "We're not goin' near Savage! We're just tryin' to keep Bandy Stevens from gettin' to 'im."

"Count me out," mumbled the taximan. "I ain't even botherin' no friends of dat Doc Savage."

"Bandy is no friend of the man," Buttons said patiently. "He don't even know Doc Savage. Nor does Savage know Bandy. Think of the two hundred bucks you're lettin' slip by not helpin' us!"

The driver licked his lips while greed and fear alternated on his wrinkled, evil face. "Yer sure I won't get messed up wit' dis bronze man?"

"Absolutely."

"Den I'll help yer," the hackey agreed.

Buttons nodded. He wheeled upon his aides. "Now listen, you rannies! We've got to work fast. I've thought of a scheme which will not only get rid of that blasted Bandy, but fix it so we won't have to worry about Doc Savage."

The others nodded uneasily.

A moment later, the men were traveling rapidly uptown in their car, with the taxicab trailing behind.

Chapter IV

THE TOUCH THAT SLEW

FORTY-SECOND STREET and Broadway had proved to be a more difficult meeting place than Bandy Stevens expected. The streets were very wide, and despite the lateness of the hour, a good deal of noisy traffic flowed—most of it taxicabs.

The hour had passed, together with an extra fifteen minutes. Bandy was worried.

"Why didn't I keep that belt on me!" he groaned. "I won't be able to give Doc Savage the low-down without them papers and maps and plans, and the letter. Blast it, anyhow!"

He peered at each taxicab which cruised past. This invariably had an embarrassing result, for the hacks always stopped, thinking he wanted to hire them. Bandy had never thought a great deal of cities, and they were dropping rapidly in his estimation.

Suddenly he discovered the vehicle for which he was waiting. He hurried to it.

"Dag-gone it, pard, I thought you was never comin'!" he grinned.

"I drove past a couple of times without seein' youse," lied the thin-necked driver. "Where's dat coin?"

Bandy passed over a hundred dollars in crisp currency. Then he dived a hand behind the rear seat cushions.

He brought out his money belt. Opening it swiftly, he saw a bulky brown envelope and a smaller white one, both apparently intact.

"Say, what's dat?" demanded the driver, pretending to be astonished at the appearance of the money belt in Bandy's hand.

"Never mind," grinned Bandy. "You can drag it, hombre. I'm through with you."

The driver let out his clutch and rolled away. He went directly to a dark, shabby street two blocks distant. Buttons Zortell waited there.

"The bow-legged runt never suspected a thing," smirked the hackey. "He looked at de envelope in de belt an' thought dey was just like he left 'em. Now I'll take de other hundred frogskins you was gonna pay me."

Buttons extended his left hand, holding currency. The driver reached for it.

Bringing his other hand into view, gripping a gun, Buttons bludgeoned the driver on the head. The man slumped. A crimson stream dribbled from his nostrils.

Buttons Zortell had been doing some thinking—and reached a conclusion. There was seven hundred dollars here—money easy for the taking. That was the kind of money Buttons liked. Six hundred of it would go on the expense account, and no one would be the wiser. Buttons's men were not in the vicinity. He had seen to that.

With swift fingers, Buttons robbed the driver.

As an afterthought, he felt of the limp man's wrist. There was no pulse. The blow had crushed the skull.

"Dead!" Buttons gulped, somewhat surprised. He squinted up and down the murky street, and was indeed glad to perceive no one in view. "Oh, well—what the heck! He ain't the first gent I've salivated."

Buttons Zortell left the vicinity, walking swiftly—but not so rapidly as to arouse suspicion. He turned southward.

THE skyscraper which housed Doc Savage's sanctum spiked up only a few blocks distant. It was for this structure that the killer headed.

Near the towering building, Buttons Zortell met one of his own men.

"Whatcha so sweaty about?" the man queried, eying his chief curiously. "You look kinda spooked."

Buttons changed the subject with an angry grunt. "How about Bandy?"

"He ain't showed up."

"Yeah? Well, he hasn't had time. He'll be here—huh! There he goes now!"

The scheming pair sidled into a convenient doorway. They could see Bandy walking, turning often to look alertly behind, toward the skyscraper entrance.

"Did you fix things for 'im?" Buttons whispered.

"I sure did!"

"Good! Bandy won't be around much longer to devil us!" Buttons chuckled fiercely. "Or Doc Savage, either! Our plan will take care of that gent!"

"He may be smart enough to see through——"

"Not a chance!"

The two fell silent, watching Bandy enter the lobby of the cloud-piercing building.

Bandy, unaware of the evil attention centered upon him, walked straight to one of the elevators which was in all-night operation.

"I'm lookin' for a jasper named Doc Savage. Got any idea where I can find 'im?"

The elevator operator smiled at Bandy's engaging cowboy drawl. "Mr. Savage is in his office on eighty-six, I believe."

The express elevator lifted Bandy to the eighty-sixth floor. He experienced no difficulty in locating the door he sought. The plain panel bore, in extremely small bronze-colored letters, the two words:

DOC SAVAGE.

Bandy discerned a push button beside the door. He thumbed it, then stepped back. Without being aware of doing so, he held his breath, wondering what manner of man this remarkable Doc Savage would be.

He was destined never to learn. His arms abruptly began to twitch, and the movement turned into a mad flailing. His eyes shut tightly in agony. His lips writhed.

"Nate Raff!" he shrieked. "Nate Raff——"

The words rattled and stuck in his throat. He sought vainly to scream again, his jaws straining wide with the frightful effort. Then, pivoting slowly as he collapsed, he slammed his length on the richly tiled corridor floor. A few spasms shook his stocky little figure, then it became slack and immobile.

Bandy had ridden his last bronc, unless they have cow ponies in the hereafter. He was dead.

THE door of Doc Savage's office whipped open an instant after Bandy had expired.

The man who stood in the opening, presented a striking figure. By his appearance alone, he would have been outstanding among any assemblage of men.

In stature, he was a giant, although proportioned with such symmetry that only his relation to the size of the door in which he stood showed his bigness. His every line—the metallic tendons of his hands, the columnar cording of his neck—denoted great physical strength. The man had the gigantic muscles of a Samson.

Bronze was his color motif. His features might have been done by some skilled sculptor in the metal, so regular were they. His hair was of a bronze a trifle darker than his skin, and it was straight, close-lying.

His eyes caught—and held—attention, above all else. They were weird, commanding eyes, like nothing so much as pools of flake gold. They radiated a hypnotic quality, an ability to inspire fear or respect—to convey threat, domination, or command. Even in repose, they glowed with the heat of an indomitable will.

He seemed, by his appearance alone, to weave a spell—this man of bronze whose fame was trickling to the far ends of the earth. He was a man, once seen, never to be forgotten—this Doc Savage.

Roving swiftly, his gaze swept the situation in the corridor, perceiving not only the body of Bandy Stevens, but also ascertaining that no one else was in sight.

Suddenly, he whipped back into his office. The speed with which he moved was amazing, for he seemed hardly to go before he was back with a strange mechanical device of chemical-filled tubes and atomizerlike spray nozzles.

The apparatus was small enough to fit compactly in the big bronze man's palm. He manipulated it an instant.

The contrivance, utilizing chemical reaction, was capable of indicating instantly the presence of poison gas in the air.

Satisfied no delay vapor was present, Doc Savage laid the device aside. He sank down beside the body and held one of the limp wrists briefly. He examined the dead man's hands. After that, he remained statuesque, quiescent.

A low, fantastic sound now filled the corridor. Mellow, trilling, the sound partook of the nature of a whistle. It was like the song of some exotic bird of the jungle, or the note of a wind filtering through a frozen forest. It was melodious, yet adhered to no particular tune.

It was part of Doc, this unique sound—a tiny, unconscious thing which he did in moments of intense concentration. His lips did not move as he made it, and it was difficult, for one not knowing, to believe the note came from Doc, such a strange essence of ventriloquism did it hold.

Doc arose and stepped to the call button beside the door. He scrutinized this.

The fact that he went directly to the push button emphasized the analytical power of his mind, his ability to discern in a minimum of time the solution of the deepest mystery.

For the call button held the explanation of Bandy Stevens's demise. It was coated with a poison so potent that a small quantity of it upon the skin would bring quick death.

DOC SAVAGE reëntered his office. The room was furnished for quiet luxury. A large safe stood against one wall, and a massive, exquisitely inlaid table shimmered in the glow of indirect lighting.

Adjoining this room was another, richly carpeted, the walls

lined with bookcases. Other ponderous volumes reposed in cabinets which stood thick on the floor.

Doc crossed this vast library to his experimental laboratory. He moved through a forest of stands and cases which held intricate chemical and electrical apparatus, and secured a bit of peculiar cloth and a stout glass jar.

With the cloth, he wiped the poison from the push button. Then he sealed the rag in the jar. Should Doc wish to analyze the poison to determine its nature, he had merely to soak the cloth in a simple chemical solution. The fabric would dissolve, leaving the poison behind, unchanged in nature, and ready for his skilled scrutiny.

A swift search of the deceased Bandy Stevens produced the well-stuffed wallet, some small change and a watch. The wallet bore Bandy's name. There were no cards or letters for identification.

Doc removed the chamois money belt, withdrew the two envelopes—one large and brown, the other small and white—and inspected them.

On each was written Doc Savage's name.

At the point of opening them, he suddenly slid both into his pockets. He glided down the corridor. He reached the endmost elevator, and a touch upon a concealed button caused the doors to open. He entered. The cage dropped like a falling rock. This was a private lift, operating with extreme speed. It made very little noise.

As he neared the street level, a sporadic series of sharp reports became louder. In the eighty-sixth-floor office, the bangings had been very faint. But Doc had heard them and recognized their nature—gunfire.

The speed elevator braked to a stop, doors opening quietly. Doc drove a swift glance at several large mirrors across the lobby. These were part of the modernistic decoration scheme—although they had been installed only after Doc became a tenant in the skyscraper. They were arranged so as to reflect the interior of the lobby to any one within the elevator cage.

Doc saw no one.

Two shots slammed noisy echoes.

The firing was outside.

An automobile engine began to moan loudly.

Two men appeared on the sidewalk. They dived headlong for a door, tore it open and pitched through. Tumbling to the tiled floor, they rolled wildly to one side, striving hurriedly to reach shelter.

A volley of lead, pursuing the men, hammered glass out

of the door. Glancing bullets screamed and chopped at the rich lobby decorations.

The car engine continued to roar. The machine flashed past the front of the great building, and sped rapidly away. After that, silence fell, proving the gunmen had fled.

THE two men who had plunged through the door, now picked themselves up. They grinned wryly at each other.

One was a huge elephant of a fellow with a severe, puritanical face. His fists were enormous, even for one of such bulk—each seemed composed of at least a gallon of flinty knuckles.

The other man was slight of build, with a somewhat unhealthy-looking complexion. He had a nervous, intense air.

The big man was Colonel John Renwick, more often known simply as "Renny." He was an engineer of ability—and fame. More than once, foreign governments had paid him fabulous fees for his services as a consulting engineer.

"Major Thomas J. Roberts," read the business cards of the pallid man. Scientific circles knew him as one of the most skilled living men in the field of electrical research. He was a wizard with the juice. He answered to the nickname of "Long Tom."

Renny and Long Tom were two of the five men who were Doc Savage's associates.

They turned their grins on Doc when he appeared.

"What was the trouble?" Doc asked. His voice was pleasant, powerful.

"Search me," Renny thumped in a tone that was like thunder gobbling in a cavern. "We came back from eating, and saw several suspicious-looking birds hanging around outside. We started over to take a squint at them—and they turned loose the fireworks."

"What became of Johnny and Ham?"

Johnny and Ham were two more of Doc's five aides.

"I guess they're outside," Renny said soberly. "They were both trying to get behind the same fire plug, the last I saw of 'em!"

Doc stepped to the widewalk.

Near the corner, two men were arguing. They had their faces shoved in close proximity, and their arms gestured heatedly.

"There they are," Renny grunted. "Squabbling over who saw that fire plug first! You see, none of us had guns."

Doc approached the pair.

"Johnny," or William Harper Littlejohn, an archæologist and geologist with few equals, was an exceedingly tall and gaunt man. His bony shoulders resembled a clothes hanger under his coat. He wore glasses, the left lens of which was a thick, powerful magnifier. Johnny's left eye had been rendered useless in the World War. Needing a magnifying glass in his work, he found it could be conveniently carried as a part of his spectacles.

Johnny scowled amiably, grumbling, "Listen, Ham, I didn't mind you trying to hog the fire plug, but I do object to being gouged with the blasted sword cane!"

"I got to the plug first!" snapped "Ham."

Ham was a dapper, wiry man, quick in his movements. His attire was sartorial perfection. The way Ham wore his clothes was a delight to the hearts of tailors. He was one of the most astute lawyers Harvard ever produced. His business cards read: "Brigadier General Theodore Marley Brooks." Quick thinking had earned him the high military commission.

Ham now sheathed the sword cane which had caused the dispute. It became an innocent black walking stick in appearance. Ham was never without it.

"What I can't understand is why that gang started shooting, with no warning!" he grumbled.

Chapter V
ARCTIC BAIT

JOHNNY examined a scratch on his gangling arm where Ham's sword cane had accidentally pricked. His wordy exchange with Ham had been entirely good-natured. It was the usual thing to argue with Ham, who had a caustic tongue and liked nothing more than a verbal tiff. Only one man could get the best of Ham in an argument, and that was "Monk"—the remaining member of Doc's group of five. Monk was not present.

"Got any idea what's up?" Ham asked Doc.

The giant bronze man produced the two envelopes which had been in Bandy Stevens's money belt. "These may give the answer."

He explained about the body in the skyscraper corridor, as the elevator lifted them.

"The dying man screamed a name just before he expired," Doc finished. "It was—Nate Raff!"

"I never heard that name before," Renny declared. "Have you fellows?"

The others shook their heads.

Doc moved the body of Bandy Stevens from the corridor floor, placing it on the inlaid office table. Before doing anything more, he called the authorities and gave the story of what had happened.

"I am taking charge of the affair," he told the police.

The official at the other end expressed satisfaction—Doc Savage and each of his five aides held honorary commissions of high rank on the New York police force. As a result of services rendered in the past, the police had standing orders to give the bronze man every coöperation. To these orders, they adhered rigidly.

The phone conversation terminated, Doc pronged the receiver. He ran a paper knife under the envelope flaps.

A letter dropped from one, a sizable bundle of paper from the other.

The men gathered around, eager to learn what the documents had to disclose. Their backs were to the large window. They gave no thought to that, however. Only one skyscraper near by was tall enough to furnish a vantage point from which an observer could see into the room. This structure lay within rifle shot—but the windows of Doc's office were of bullet-proof glass.

No danger seemed likely to reach them from the nearby building.

HAD DOC or his men turned powerful binoculars on the tower of the skyscraper a few blocks distant, they might have detected something of interest. This tower, thrusting upward not unlike a candle, was equipped as an observation point. By payment of a small sum, any one could have the privilege of surveying the city from the lofty perch, at any hour of the day or night.

Nickel-in-the-slot telescopes were mounted on the platform, to permit patrons a better view of the metropolis spread out below them.

Buttons Zortell and one of his hirelings had their eyes jammed to these telescopes. They were getting an excellent view of what happened in Doc Savage's office.

"The scheme is workin'!" Buttons chuckled. "Them hombres will never guess the truth!"

"Yeah—we've got 'em goin'!" the other man agreed.

"Small thanks to you!" Buttons snapped.

"Aw-w—whatcha beefin' about?"

"About the boner you pulled down on the street a while ago—you sap! When Doc Savage's four men walked toward us, it was you who started throwin' lead!"

The man reddened angrily. "I figured they had tumbled to our game!"

"Yeah? Well, I don't think they had. They just saw us standin' there like a bunch of spooky mavericks, and come over to see what ailed us."

"We made a mistake in hangin' around there."

"You're tellin' me?" Buttons snorted irately. "What a mess of bum shootin' we done! I don't think we even nicked anybody!"

"Them fellers moved like they had been shot at before," complained the other. "They popped out of sight like prairie dogs."

"Havin' 'em bump into us didn't do any harm, after all, I guess," Buttons said in a speculative tone. "In fact, it fits in fine with the rest of my scheme."

Several seconds of silence followed, while both men concentrated on watching the tableau in Doc Savage's office.

"They're sure takin' their time readin' that letter," Buttons muttered.

His companion laughed uneasily. "Are you plumb certain you didn't make a mistake an' stick the genuine papers back in the envelopes?"

"Of course not!" Nevertheless, Buttons hastily drew a bundle of documents from the side pocket of his coat and inspected them. "Nope. I didn't make a mistake."

He returned to his pocket the original contents of Bandy Stevens's money belt.

"We can't kill no more time here," he declared. "Now is our chance to go ahead with our scheme. All of Doc Savage's men are with him but one. That one is a bird who looks like a gorilla. I found out from the newspapers I called that he's known as 'Monk' on account of his looks. His name is Lieutenant Colonel Andrew Blodgett Mayfair. Some handle for a gent as homely as he is!"

"How'll we find 'im?"

"That's easy! The newspapers gave me his business address. He's a famous chemist, with a hang-out, where he works, down near Wall Street."

"Wall Street—huh?" grinned the other man. "I've always wanted to see that place."

"You'll see it!" Buttons rumbled ominously. "This Monk rannihan is gonna see somethin', too—somethin' he won't like. He's probably workin' all night, too."

The two hastily quitted their lofty perch.

IN DOC Savage's office, scrutiny of the envelope contents was still under way. The letter came first. It was addressed to Doc, and read:

DEAR MR. SAVAGE: I have heard a lot about you, and how you go to bat for fellers who are in trouble. I sure need some help, so I'm taking the liberty of sending my pal, Bandy Stevens, to ask your assistance.

I'm sure your aid will make things come out all right, and I can pay you just about any amount of money you want for your services.

Here's the layout: A few weeks ago, I was prospecting and found a big vein of radium. I panned out enough to get money for placer mining machinery.

Selling the radium, several ounces of it, must have tipped off somebody, because right away I began having troubles. A gang is after me. I don't know 'em. But right now, as I write this, they have me cornered in my cabin forty-five miles west of Fort Caribou, in the Hudson Bay country of Canada.

I'm inclosing a map showing where my cabin and the radium mine is. My friend Bandy Stevens will try to get to you, but my enemies will probably try to stop him, and try to keep you from helping me. Bandy will tell you more.

Please, Mr. Savage, won't you give a man a hand?

BEN JOHNSON.

Strange little lights flickered in Doc Savage's golden eyes as he ended perusal of the missive.

They examined the map next. It was an ordinary variety —probably half the large news stands in New York sold them.

On it, a pair of crosses were carefully inked.

"Well, well!" Long Tom kneaded his rather pallid hands. "Some one has insulted us, by thinking we would fall for this fake."

BUTTONS ZORTELL would have been shocked, had he witnessed the quickness with which Doc Savage's crew had discovered the documents were spurious. Unbounded surprise would have been his, for he had taken great pains— even to spelling every word correctly—in faking them.

"The writer of the letter made a glaring error in mentioning the radium," Doc announced. "Radium is not panned from ore, but extracted with costly and intricate machinery. Furthermore, he says he sold several ounces of the rare substance. That is a tremendous quantity—for radium. Enough to have a pronounced effect on the market! No such sale was made recently."

"That's right," agreed Renny, whose engineering knowledge made him familiar with the subject.

"Second, that letter was written hardly more than an hour ago," Doc continued. "The ink is still somewhat damp."

"Too bad," Ham grumbled. "I'd like to go up North. A vacation in the Canadian woods appeals to me."

"My guess is that it will take us to Arizona," Doc told him.

Ham betrayed surprise at this. Then, to show he was capable of detective work himself, he stepped over and examined Bandy Stevens's coat.

"You win, Doc," he admitted. "This suit came from a Phoenix, Arizona, clothier."

Doc scrutinized the features of the dead man.

"Wind has reddened the fellow's face," he pointed out. "A protected area about the eyes indicates goggles were worn. That means an open plane."

"Then it would seem he came from Arizona to New York by plane," Ham grunted.

"We don't know he came here from Arizona!" Renny objected. "He might actually have come from the Hudson Bay country."

Doc turned out the cuff's of Bandy's trousers, disclosing a small amount of lint and several crumpled fragments of grayish leaves.

"Leaves off sagebrush," he indicated. "Not greatly withered, either. They were shaken off as the man walked through sagebrush not more than twenty-four hours ago. I think we can rest assured he flew straight here from Arizona."

Doc now rifled through New York telephone books, and the ponderous city directories. He did not find what he sought.

"I was looking for the name of Nate Raff—the name Bandy Stevens cried out as he died," he explained. "There is no such person listed."

Ham glanced at his watch. "Monk will want to be in on this. What say we call him?"

Doc nodded. Striding to a desk, he flipped one of five small switches.

On the desk stood what seemed to be a box with a frosted glass panel in one end. As Doc moved the switch, a movie-like image appeared on the panel.

This mechanism was a telephone-television apparatus of Doc's construction. The five switches connected to circuits that led to the places of business of Doc's five men— a switch for each man.

On the scanning screen of the televisor appeared the interior of Monk's laboratory in a penthouse atop an office building near Wall Street.

The laboratory was untenanted.

"MONK probably hasn't come to work yet," Ham decided. "He'll be there soon. The big mug has a habit of going to work at five o'clock in the morning. It's almost that time now."

"You've got a lot of room to talk about working hours," snorted Johnny. "You've been up here all night."

"But only to watch you birds sweat!" Ham retorted.

This was hardly the truth. Ham had taken a part in the night's work, which was the tedious task of perfecting plans and structural details for an addition to a strange institution which Doc Savage maintained in up-State New York. Few people knew of this weird place, or the fantastic purpose it served, and should the knowledge have gotten out, it would have proven sensational.

For it was to this institution that Doc sent such criminals as he captured. Once incarcerated there, they underwent delicate brain operations which wiped out all knowledge of their past, leaving their minds a blank.

Then they received an intensive education, not only in right living and good citizenship, but also in the art of making an honest living. They were taught to hate criminals and their ways. No man, once released from this place, had ever returned to a life of crime.

Doc's money maintained the unusual "college," and the specialists who performed the operations had been taught by his hand.

Gathering up the plans upon which they had worked through most of the night, Doc placed them in the great safe.

"We'll attend to these later," he declared. "They are almost complete, anyway."

Ham stared grimly at the lifeless form of Bandy Stevens. "Have you any idea who did this, Doc?"

The bronze man replied with a question, "Did you notice anything in particular about the men who shot at you downstairs?"

"They were sunburned fellows; that could easily be noticed," Ham replied.

"And all of them but one used single-action six-shooters," Renny boomed.

"That type of gun is the standard firearm of the West," Doc pointed out. "They were evidently Westerners. Bandy

Stevens was from the West. So that points to a connection between them and his killing."

"I'll bet they were the murderers!" snapped Ham. "When we walked toward them, they thought they were discovered. That's why they started shooting."

Doc nodded. He moved to his televisiphone and threw the switch. "I'll try to get Monk again."

THE interior of Monk's laboratory once more appeared on the scanning screen. The great racks of chemicals, retorts and test tubes showed with a fair degree of distinctness.

The laboratory was now occupied.

An extremely pretty blond young woman approached the mechanism. She was tall, exquisitely formed. As she came closer, the televisor screen framed her features, picture-fashion. The greater detail only accentuated her beauty. She was a knock-out!

The blonde was Lea Aster, Monk's secretary. Monk was wont to boast he had the prettiest secretary in New York, and he probably did not exaggerate.

Doc spoke into a microphone which was part of the mechanism. "Is Monk there?"

"Not yet," Lea Aster's voice, rich and modulated as finely as the tones of a high-salaried radio singer, came from a loudspeaker built into the televisor. "He hasn't come in yet."

"Have him give us a look when he arrives," Doc replied.

"Certainly—but wait! I hear some one at the door now. Perhaps it is Monk."

The young woman turned from the televisiphone. Since she was no longer before the "eye" of the apparatus, Doc and his men could see the door of Monk's laboratory.

A man suddenly appeared in the opening. He was huge, burly, vicious of feature. Two bullet scars were like gray buttons, one on either cheek.

It was Buttons Zortell!

"That's one of the birds who jumped us on the street!" Renny boomed. Then he fell silent, watching the tableau in Monk's workshop.

Dashing forward, Buttons Zortell seized Lea Aster. The blonde screamed, struck at him.

Facing the televisor, she shrilled, "Help!"

More men appeared in the laboratory—confederates of Buttons Zortell.

"Smash that box of a jigger!" Buttons ordered angrily.

One of the men ran over and bashed at the televisiphone box with a heavy six-gun.

The image vanished as the mechanism was put out of commission.

Chapter VI

MONK IN TROUBLE

LEA ASTER was an athletic young woman. The roof outside the penthouse held a screened-in tennis court, and few days passed that she and Monk did not play a few hard-fought sets of the game.

She was inflicting punishment on Buttons Zortell. She hit him on the Adam's apple, a blow Monk had shown her with the assurance that it was one of the most painful that can be landed.

Buttons squawked in agony.

"Gimme a hand!" he bawled at his hirelings. "This heifer is gonna ruin me!"

The others rushed to his aid.

They were half across the laboratory when the tornado hit them. The tornado was Monk—two hundred and sixty pounds of him. He had arrived at the opportune moment.

His arms, hairy and corded and inches longer than his legs, gathered two men in a fond, terrible hug. He squeezed. Both victims blared out screams of pain. Their agony could not have been greater had they been pinned under a locomotive.

Another man swept up a chair, swung it down atop Monk's head. But Monk's bullet of a skull seemed to disappear, turtlewise, in his sloping, mountainous shoulders as he ducked. The chair shattered, fragments flying over the laboratory.

"Ye-o-w!" howled Monk, more from rage than pain. He spun and hooked a foot expertly, causing the chair wielder to crash to the floor.

Monk slammed the pair in his arms atop the fellow who had fallen. All three lay in a feebly squirming pile, too stunned to care what else happened.

Monk rushed Buttons Zortell.

Buttons saw his danger. He released Lea Aster and pawed for his six-guns. Seeing he could never get them in time, he dived for the door.

He did not make it. Monk's furry hands snatched him up as though he were a fleeing rooster. Buttons rained blows with his fists, kicked, bit savagely. But he was helpless against the prodigious strength of the gorilla of a man who held him.

Monk hugged him, and began putting on pressure.

"Don't kill me!" Buttons screamed in mortal terror. "Please——" There was no air in his chest for him to say more. His face purpled.

Monk, aware two more men remained on their feet in the room, whirled—never releasing the ghastly pressure on Buttons. He stopped suddenly. A blank look overspread his homely face.

"That's right!" snarled a man. "Drop Buttons, or we'll let the mohairrie have a dose of lead!"

The pair had cornered Lea Aster. One was holding a gun to her head.

Monk hesitated, on the horns of a bitter dilemma.

"Quick!" roared one of the two who held the girl.

Monk could read purpose on a human face. He saw they intended to shoot his secretary if he resisted. The features of both men were twisted with the will to slay.

Monk dropped Buttons Zortell and put up his hands.

THE men closed in on him with a rush, their elated cries like the barking of mongrels.

Lea Aster, the instant she was released, sprang upon Buttons Zortell. The force of her charge knocked the man to the floor. They scuffled violently until they were separated.

"Whew!" mumbled Buttons, eying her wryly. "I never before seen a female critter as violent as you are!"

Lea Aster kicked the man holding her. He gasped, then flung her into a corner.

Monk, watching his secretary, distinctly saw her shove something into hiding behind an apparatus cabinet.

Buttons booted the three who still lay on the floor. They weaved to their feet, still hardly able to navigate.

A man jabbed Monk with a single-action six. "What're we gonna do with big hairy, here?"

"I'd like to poison 'im with lead!" Buttons snarled. "But he ain't no account to us as a corpse! We gotta take 'im along."

"I wish we'd picked a different one of Doc Savage's gang!" groaned a man. "If you ask me, I think we tackled the wild steer of the lot!"

"Get goin'!" snapped Buttons.

"What about the mohairrie?"

For answer, Buttons suddenly rushed Lea Aster. He fought with the blonde young woman an instant, then succeeded in knocking her unconscious with a fist blow.

"That'll hold her," he grated. "And it pays her back for the whammin' she handed me."

Monk surged forward angrily as the blonde dropped, but four gun snouts gouging into his massive chest caused him to change his mind. Getting himself shot would not help his blonde secretary.

"Drift!" Buttons ordered.

Meekly, Monk permitted himself to be led out of the building. His captors had their car parked near by. He was forced to enter and occupy the center of the rear seat.

THE car rolled slowly through traffic. At this early hour, few vehicles other than delivery trucks were on the streets.

"Mind telling me what I'm headed for?" Monk asked. His voice was so peacefully mild that it seemed comical coming from one of his hairy bulk.

"Shut up or I'll feed you this hogleg!" snarled one of the men, jamming a big six-gun into Monk's face with a hasty motion.

Buttons Zortell bestowed a knowing wink on a fellow beside him, then turned to face Monk.

"It won't hurt you to know what you're in for," he smirked. "We're gonna use you to keep Doc Savage from mixin' in our business. To put it plainer, if Doc don't behave himself, we're gonna scrag you."

"How lovely!" Monk said with deceptive gentleness.

Buttons blinked and drew back a little, remembering the terrible clutch of Monk's furry paws. He could see Monk was not scared in the least, which was not to his liking.

"This ain't somethin' to act sassy about!" he told Monk fiercely. "A gent named Ben Johnson has a radium mine up in the Hudson Bay country, and we're after it. Johnson sent to Doc Savage for help. We're dead serious about this. If Savage interferes, we're gonna croak you. We're gonna notify Savage of that, right away."

Monk listened to this with much interest. It was the first he had heard of a radium mine. He considered it stupid of his captors to tell him about it in this voluntary fashion.

"Where's it located?" he asked. "The radium mine, I mean."

Buttons and his helpers exchanged knowing looks. "We ain't sayin', hombre."

Monk settled back, his bulk crowding the men on either side of him. He marked the fact that the men were Westerners, but did not mention it to them.

Monk's eyes were small, twinkling stars in their pits of gristle. His bullet of a head did not seem to hold room for more than a spoonful of brains. His appearance was deceptive. Monk had performed miracles in the field of chemical research during his career. Moreover, his wits were far from sluggish.

This was not the first time Monk had been in a tight spot—Doc Savage and his men walked often in the shadow of deadly peril. Past experience had taught Monk it was a good thing to have a trick always up his sleeve.

Apparently greatly worried, Monk began to bite his finger nails. When he had given the fingers of one hand a thorough nibbling, he changed to the other. This nibbling continued several seconds.

In the meantime, Buttons Zortell had suddenly started feeling through his pockets. His face showed alarm. His fingers flew desperately in and out of his clothing.

"Them papers!" he gulped. "They're gone!"

"What papers?" a man asked him.

"The ones that were in——" Buttons bit off the rest. He had just made the disquieting discovery that he no longer possessed the documents taken from Bandy Stevens's money belt, but he did not want his prisoner to know.

Monk noted the byplay. He smiled in a small, secret way. He remembered how his pretty secretary had made a gesture of hiding something in the laboratory—he felt certain Lea Aster had slipped the missing documents from Buttons's pockets. She was a clever girl.

For several seconds, Monk kneaded his fingers together. Then, as though tired, he slouched over against the man riding on his left.

Monk's eyes were tightly closed.

He repeated the slumping procedure with the guards on his right, his eyes still pinched shut.

Both guards suddenly yelled, dropped their guns and pawed at their eyes.

Without opening his own lids, Monk took a flying leap out of the slow-moving car. He hit the pavement, running. Opening his eyes, he dived for the handiest shelter, an alleyway.

He popped into it before the first shot thundered behind him. His captors had been taken completely by surprise.

MONK snorted gleefully as he ran. Under his finger nails he had carried caked deposits of several chemicals—he wore his nails long for that sole purpose. Dampened and mixed, the compounds gave off a potent form of tear gas.

"Doc himself couldn't have done it any better!" Monk chortled as he increased his speed.

As a matter of truth, it was from Doc that Monk had copied the tear-gas trick.

Glancing upward, Monk discovered a fire-escape landing. He leaped, caught it and hauled himself up. With an elbow, he pushed the glass out of the first window he came to. Bullets jangled noisily on the fire escape and gun sound cascaded deafeningly in the alleyway. Monk lunged through the window, escaping the deadly hail.

He found himself in a bedroom. A man came out of a bath adjoining, his face half lathered, a heavy shaving mug in one hand. He threw the mug at the invader.

Monk ducked it easily. He made for a door. It was unlocked, and let him out into a hallway that reeked cooking odors. He descended a flight of stairs, taking his time.

More shooting broke out before he reached the street. Once outside, he discovered a cop had come upon the scene. Buttons Zortell and his henchmen had fled, after swapping a few bullets with the policeman. No one had been hit.

Monk lost several minutes in soothing the irate apartment dweller whose window he had smashed. He paid for the window, as well as for the shaving mug, which had been broken when the man threw it at him.

Hailing a taxi, he rode back to his office. He was paying the driver when Doc Savage hurried out of the building, accompanied by his four aides. They had just been up to the penthouse, and they were uneasy.

"You guys can wipe the worry off your pans," Monk grinned at them. "Everything is all right."

"Everything?" Renny demanded. "Is——"

"Sure. It's all hunky-dory. And, say—I found out what was behind it. A fella named Ben Johnson has a radium mine up North. He wants your help, Doc, and these guys are tryin' to keep him from gettin' it."

Ham laughed nastily. "So you were dumb enough to fall for that sap story?"

Monk gave the dapper little sword-cane-carrying lawyer a look of injured innocence.

"Aw—go steal a pig!" he grunted.

Ham purpled. His fists clenched. He seemed about ready to explode inwardly.

Monk had only to mention pigs, hogs, or anything connected with pork to get Ham's goat. This state of affairs harkened back to the World War. Ham, as a practical joke, had taught Monk several very insulting French words, telling him they were the proper words to curry the favor of a French general. Monk had tried it—and landed in the guardhouse.

He had only been out a few days when Ham, then known only as Brigadier General Brooks, had been hailed up before a court-martial on a charge of stealing hams. From that day, he was called Ham. He had never been able to prove Monk had framed him, and that irked his lawyer soul.

Ham shook his sword cane at Monk. "One of these days, I'm gonna give you a close shave with this sword! A shave right down to your bones!"

MONK snorted and gave his attention to Doc. "Do you think they fed me a phony story, Doc?"

"They probably did," Doc told him. "For some reason, they seem to want us to dash off for the Hudson Bay country on a wild-goose chase."

"Then why'd they kidnap me?"

"Merely to make their story look better. They wished to impress me with their opposition to my going North—hoping that would only make my determination the firmer. They are very clever."

"Yeah. I should've known they were acting too stupid when they told me about the radium mine. I reckon they intended to hold me a few hours, then let me escape. They gimme the mine story so I'd carry it to you."

"They're taking great pains to get us out of the city," Renny put in. "Why is that?"

"You're wasting time asking Monk that," clipped Ham, still smarting from the pig reference. "He wouldn't know —the missing link."

Monk grinned from ear to ear. "You don't say! You little shyster—I'll bet I can cast a lot of light on the mystery!"

"How?"

"The leader of the gang—Buttons, his pals called him— was carryin' some kind of papers. My secretary snitched 'em."

"So what?"

"So what d'you think? My secretary has got 'em upstairs."

A hot, startled light came into Doc's golden eyes. His men swapped blank looks.

"We misunderstood you, Monk," Doc said steadily. "When you said everything was all right, we took it to mean both you and your secretary were safe!"

Monk seemed about to choke. "What d'you mean?"

"Lea Aster is not in your laboratory!"

Chapter VII
NICK CLIPTON

MONK's homely face set in a rock-like mask. His big, amiable mouth warped a grim scowl.

"But she was left behind when they took me away!" he muttered. "Buttons knocked her out. He didn't hit her hard enough to do any serious damage, though."

Doc wheeled back into the building, saying, "we'll go up and look again for her!"

A red flush of sunlight suffused the penthouse which contained Monk's laboratory, although the street below was still somewhat gloomy. Sunbeams, sloping into the workroom itself, were reflected dazzlingly from the myriads of glass test tubes, bottles, pestles, and from metallic stands of mechanisms. It was as though the room were heaped with scintillating jewelry.

Monk's sharp eyes detected several stands of apparatus lying upon the floor—stands which had been upright when his captors forced him from the laboratory.

"Did you fellows upset those?" he asked, indicating the fallen apparatus on the floor.

"No," Doc assured him.

Monk groaned. "They have been upset since I was taken away. It looks like there was another fight in here."

"You say it was a light blow which knocked Lea Aster unconscious?"

"Yes. She must have come to." Monk shook a fist angrily. "It looks like Buttons and his gang rushed back here after I got away from them and grabbed my secretary. Don't you think that's what happened, Doc?"

"Apparently," Doc admitted.

Monk now hurried to the apparatus cabinet behind which Lea Aster had concealed something. He searched, but found nothing.

"If the girl actually did slip the documents from Buttons's pocket and hide them here, they've been taken," he said thoughtfully. "It is possible Miss Aster regained consciousness, secured the papers, and had them when Buttons returned."

Ham had been standing quietly to one side, slowly tapping an immaculate shoe toe with the tip of his sword cane. His high, intelligent forehead was wrinkled from hard thinking. "What I cannot understand is why they came back for the young woman!" he declared. "Granting that they're trying to send us up North on a wild-goose chase, it seems to me they should be satisfied that they have us bluffed. The elaborate scheming they're doing to get us out of town shows they know we're bad fellows to monkey with. Why should they draw our vengeance further by seizing the girl?"

"I have a surmise that explains both questions," Doc told him. "Buttons realized he must have lost the papers in this laboratory. He came back for them, and discovered Lea Aster reading them. He was forced to take the young woman, because she had learned the contents of the documents."

Doc and his men now questioned the single elevator operator on duty in the building at this early hour, in an effort to verify the correctness of their reasoning. But that individual had seen no one leave with Monk's secretary in tow.

"They could have come and gone by the stairs without being observed—they had enough time," Doc pointed out.

Back in the laboratory, they continued their consultation.

"We're sure of one thing"—Renny rumbled in a voice that threatened to shake apparatus off stands—"the fact that they're trying to decoy us into Canada."

"Well, they won't have any luck at that!" Ham snapped.

The words were hardly off his lips when he started violently.

Doc's strange trilling note had sounded unexpectedly. It came into being, seemingly from nowhere. Awesome, melodious, its eerie nature defying description, it rose and fell. Only a moment did it last, then it trailed away.

"What is it, Doc?" Ham barked out quickly.

Doc did not reply with words. He leveled an arm at the city telephone, which stood on a table near them. The receiver was off the hook and resting on the table top.

Moving to the instrument swiftly, Doc pressed the receiver to his ear. He heard sounds of a man breathing. These persisted several seconds.

Long Tom sprinted out of the laboratory, intent on getting to another phone and having the connection to this instrument traced. He was not successful in that, however.

Buttons Zortell was the man at the other end of the phone wire. Something of the sudden tension which had seized the laboratory was transmitted to him. He became alarmed. Hanging up quickly, he quitted the booth from which he had been listening and hurried outside.

The booth was in a drug store less than a block from the building which supported Monk's penthouse. Buttons joined his men, who were waiting in their parked car in a side street.

"What'd you learn, Buttons?" quizzed one of the men.

"Plenty!" their leader snarled. "Them hombres are wise that the radium mine in Canada is all a fake! I don't savvy how they got next to our scheme! I figured we'd put it over plumb slick!"

"Blazes! Have they found out why we want 'em out of New York?"

"Not yet!" Buttons muttered uneasily.

THE flyer with the white mustache and eyebrows took the wheel. The car moved off. The men sat back pretending nonchalance, but keeping wary eyes on each policeman they passed. They were nervous, for Lea Aster, securely bound and gagged was on the floor of the car. And none were less settled of mind than Buttons Zortell.

"This Doc Savage and his men are a sharp bunch!" he growled. "Listenin' at the phone, I could hear pretty much all they said. It was a darn good phone, and they musta been standin' close to it. They stood there and reasoned out exactly what happened when we came back huntin' them papers. They even figured we'd grabbed the mohairrie because she'd read the papers."

"That's sure what happened," a man agreed.

"Go to our hotel," Buttons commanded the driver. "I've gotta get in touch with the boss. This thing is gettin' too much for me."

The men reached their hotel without incident.

Leaving the others to wait in the car, Buttons entered the hostelry and hurried to his room. He lost no time putting in a long-distance telephone call to Arizona. The wire connections he obtained were excellent; the conversation passed back and forth clearly.

Buttons recited all that had occurred. He sought to color the story in a fashion which made his accomplishments sound sizable, and his mistakes unimportant.

"I figure I've done a pretty good job, boss!" he finished.

"The hell you have!" gritted the distant master mind. "You've bungled right and left! Where are you talking from?"

"My hotel," Buttons said sourly.

"Of all the nitwits! Didn't you ever hear of telephone operators listenin' in?"

"That won't hurt nothin'!"

"Maybe not. But it would have, had you called me under my right name, instead of Nick Clipton. From now on, never get in touch with me except by the name of Nick Clipton. Savvy?"

"I gotcha."

"Furthermore, check out of that hotel the instant you hang up! Make sure nobody can trace you!"

"All right," Buttons promised sheepishly.

"And you're leaving New York right away! You're not needed there any more!"

"What about the mohairrie?"

"The girl—tie a rock to her neck and throw her in the river!"

Buttons swallowed. Callous as he was, this talk of outright murder of a woman shocked him.

"You say I ain't needed in New York any more?" he questioned nervously. "What does that mean?"

"It means I've taken care of everything from this end!" snapped the distant man masquerading under the name of Nick Clipton. "The rest of the boys have been workin' under my orders. The thing for you to do is get back here and forget Doc Savage."

"The trouble is, he ain't gonna forget us!" Buttons muttered.

"You think he suspects the Western angle?"

"I ain't sure. It wouldn't surprise me none."

The long phone circuit rattled the distant man's profane exclamation. "Then maybe we'd better put Savage and his gang out of the way."

"That won't be easy to do."

"Dry up. Let me think for a minute."

BUTTONS could hear his own watch ticking noisily in the silence which followed. In the street below, cars honked. The morning sun had already made the hotel room warm, stuffy.

"Have you still got the various devices I gave you?" asked the man in Arizona.

"All but the poison fangs for the dog, and the poison that'll kill you if you touch it. I used them two on Bandy Stevens. They were numbers one and two on the list."

"Have you got No. 3?"

"Sure."

"Find a suitable place and use it. You can figure out the details, can't you?"

"Yeah," Buttons replied uneasily.

"All right. That will dispose of Doc Savage. It can't fail."

"Um-m!" said Buttons doubtfully. "And you want me to scrag the mohairrie, huh?"

"Exactly."

"Listen, boss—supposin' we just hold her until Doc Savage is out of the way. If somethin' should go wrong, and we didn't get rid of 'im, we might keep 'im off our necks by threatenin' to croak her."

The distant man considered this at length.

"Do it that way, then," he agreed finally. "Keep her alive. And let's end this talk—it has probably cost me fifty bucks already. Are you sure you can lead Doc Savage into a trap?"

"Plump positive I can!" Buttons declared. "I already got a swell scheme in mind."

"Good. If it works, get rid of the girl and come on back to Arizona. If it don't work, come on back anyhow—but fetch the girl alive. When you get here, hole up in the Red Skull hangout."

"Shall we come by plane?"

"Of course."

"But Whitey's sky chariot was burned——"

"Buy another. Steal a plane, if you have to."

"Whitey don't know the location of the Red Skull joint."

"You sap! You can tell 'im where it is, can't you? And we've done enough lallygaggin'! So long!"

This terminated the conversation.

Striding to an assortment of baggage at one side of the hotel room, Buttons selected a huge Gladstone. He carried this piece of luggage with him as he left the hostelry.

His men greeted him with anxious queries. "What's the boss say, Buttons?"

"Don't ask so blasted many questions!" he snarled peevishly. "I'll tell you when the time comes. We got a job ahead of us that's gonna take some expert handlin'!"

Buttons wanted peace in which to mull over his evil plan. It would take careful preparation and execution. But the scheme was diabolical in its cleverness. Buttons began to experience a glow of satisfaction. The more he thought about it, the less possibility could he see of the plot failing.

Doc Savage and his five men were finally to be disposed of, Buttons felt positive. The thought made him smirk with satisfaction.

Chapter VIII

DEATH DECOY

BUTTONS ZORTELL would have experienced doubts had he been sitting in on what was transpiring in Monk's penthouse laboratory. Buttons's long-distance telephone call to Arizona was not the only one.

Doc Savage was in touch with the editor of the leading

Phoenix newspaper. He was seeking to learn something of the individual whose name Bandy Stevens had cried out in his death throes—Nate Raff.

"Nate Raff!" repeated the editor, after Doc had put his query. "Do you mean 'Tough Nate' Raff, president of the Mountain Desert Construction Company? He's the only Nate Raff I know of."

"Can you tell me something about him?" Doc requested.

"What do you want to know?"

"Everything. How did he get his name—Tough Nate?"

"Simply because he's plenty hard. Construction men out in this country have hair on their chests. Nate Raff is the furriest of the lot. He's a man-driver, and he has a sharp business head."

"Is he honest?"

"As far as I know. The Mountain Desert Construction Company is a three-partner concern. But Tough Nate runs it, though."

"Who are the other partners?"

"Richard O'Melia is one. He is construction superintendent, in charge of actual work. O'Melia has killed a man or two in his time—but he may be honest enough. He didn't go to the pen for any of the killings.

"The other partner is Ossip Keller, the brains of the lot. He handles surveys, cost estimates, and makes the detailed plans of all their jobs."

"You seem to know a great deal about these men," Doc suggested. "Have they been in the news recently?"

"I'll say! They're throwing a big power dam across the upper end of Red Skull Canyon. They got a lot of publicity because they're financing themselves. They're building the dam, using only their own money, for the avowed purpose of keeping their employees at work. I don't think it's entirely generosity on their part, though. They hope to make the dam pay by selling electrical power."

"Any scandal connected with the enterprise?"

"Not that I've heard. Why do you ask that?"

"Merely curious."

"Say—what did you say your name is? I didn't catch it."

"Doc Savage."

An explosive ejaculation came over the wire. The newspaper editor demanded eagerly: "What's up? Be a sport and give me the low-down!"

"What makes you think there is a low-down?"

"There must be! Tough Nate Raff left Phoenix last night on the regular passenger plane. He told one of our reporters he was going to New York to see you—Doc Savage!"

"That is news to me," Doc said dryly.

Before the conversation could continue, there was some kind of a commotion in the distant newspaper office, during which several voices shouted and the editor left the phone. Doc could not catch the words.

The Arizona editor suddenly returned to the phone. He was excited.

"The passenger plane in which Tough Nate Raff was riding, crashed in flames in New Mexico!" he shouted. "Everybody aboard was killed! We just got the flash over the press wires!"

HALF an hour later, Doc Savage was reading an account of the tragedy in the latest editions of the New York newspapers. The sheets had hit the streets quickly with the news.

He obtained one noteworthy bit of information—the bodies of those aboard the ill-fated air liner had been burned beyond identification.

Cause of the fire and crash was unknown, as yet. A government aëronautical inspector was en route to the scene to investigate. A horse wrangler on a ranch, while engaged at his early morning task, had come upon the wreckage. The sound of a crash during the night had awakened cowboys on the ranch, but they had dismissed this as the wrangler's pony kicking the corral bars. The sound, however, placed the hour of the disaster at about three o'clock in the morning.

According to this time, the plane had been flying nearly an hour behind its usual schedule.

The craft had struck in a canyon, which accounted for the flames not being seen.

"There is nothing to indicate foul play in connection with the wreck—as yet," Doc remarked.

Monk muttered, "I'd like to lay a bet with somebody that the plane was crashed to murder Tough Nate Raff."

"There is no proof."

"Maybe not. But the wreck is too much of a coincidence."

"It might be wise to remember the plane was almost an hour behind schedule when disaster befell it," Doc suggested.

Monk eyed Doc questioningly, but the big bronze man did not amplify his statement, or even give his reasons for making the remark. Monk would like to have heard an explanation. Doc had a faculty for picking out suspicious circumstances which later proved significant.

A bit later, the telephone rang.

Monk answered it—and emitted a squawl of delight.

"It's my secretary!" he shouted, then barked into the phone: "Are you safe?"

"No!" the young woman said rapidly. "I'm still a prisoner! But this phone was behind a box, and they didn't notice it. They don't know I'm talking."

"Where are you?"

"In a vacant tenement building on Seashore Street. I saw the number—it's 1113. I'm on the ground floor. The whole building is empty. Can you come—sh-h-h! My guard is returning, I think."

A sharp click denoted the replacing of the distant receiver.

Slamming down his own instrument, Monk lumbered for the door. Doc and the others trailed him. In the elevator going down, Monk gave them the text of the conversation.

"We may be able to nab the whole gang!" Monk chortled. His homely features were a network of grin wrinkles. He was more elated than he would have let his friends know—especially the sharp-tongued Ham, who was always riding him anyway. Monk thought a lot of his attractive blonde secretary. She was the most efficient young woman he had met, and one of the prettiest.

There was another reason why she had a big hold on his affections—she liked Monk. This was no small item, considering how homely Monk was. Monk's features were so pleasantly ugly they scared most young ladies.

In truth, Monk was more than a little in love with Lea Aster. He did not admit this, though, even to himself. The mere thought of settling down to the peaceful existence of a married man made Monk shiver. Excitement and danger had become a necessity with the homely fellow. Without them he would be a fish out of water.

They wedged into a taxicab for their ride—with the exception of Doc Savage, who rode outside on the running board, where his sharp eyes kept a lookout for danger. This was a procedure Doc habitually followed when trouble threatened. Too, his mighty bronze form was a living badge, which insured police noninterference.

Such a badge was needed in the wild rush of their cab across town. They would not have gotten many blocks without it, for they broke all speed laws.

THE eleven hundred block on Seashore Street was walled with five and six-story tenement buildings. Yet no soul resided within the confines of the block. The structures were shabby and had long since lived out their usefulness. A building corporation had bought the real estate, as well as all leases, and had ordered tenants out. Soon the structures would be razed to make room for a modern apartment development.

Doc and his men quitted their cab two blocks from the spot. Monk, grim and anxious, started forward. Doc halted him.

"Wait."

Monk swallowed his impatience and rejoined the group. Long ago, he had learned the wisdom of obeying Doc's slightest wish. Not that Doc was a stickler for discipline—it was simply that the reasons for what he did were always sound.

Leaving the others behind, Doc advanced alone.

He did not go near the front door of 1113, the house where Lea Aster had said she was being held. Instead, he scaled a low fence and entered a series of filthy courts behind the buildings.

Never showing himself to the windows of 1113, Doc entered an adjacent tenement. Rickety stairs led him upward and a squeaking hatch let him out on the roof. He crossed to the roof of the structure Lea Aster had named. A skylight gave under his sharp tug.

He swung through, dropped. His landing was noiseless, padded by the spring of tremendous leg muscles.

No sound met his ears. He moved down, a bronze ghost of a figure in the murky halls and stairways. The building could not have been emptied of its tenants more than a few days ago, since telephones had not yet been removed. But already it reeked the ratty smell of age.

Paint and paper was scabby on the walls. Patches of plaster had fallen, scattering gray fragments which would crunch loudly if stepped upon.

Doc reached the fourth floor, descended to the third, then the second. No stirrings, no conversation, reached him. Somewhere a lump of plaster fell noisily. Rats scampered. Outside, the traffic on near-by streets made muffled murmurs.

A metallic wraith, Doc glided halfway down the flight of stairs that led to the ground floor. He paused and listened. His hearing was trained, sharp.

He caught the tick of a watch. The sound was rapid, indicating by its speed a woman's wrist watch.

Doc knew Lea Aster always wore a small timepiece upon her wrist.

THE ticking emanated from a large room opening off the foot of the staircase. Doc did not approach this chamber at once, but stood in the lower hallway for several moments.

He went to the front door, moving slowly, his golden

eyes roving steadily. Through a door, and across a room at the side, he saw a box on the floor. There was dust on the floor of the room, and this bore marks which instantly told him the young woman prisoner had been kept there for a time.

Doc approached the box. Behind it was a telephone. He lifted the box. There was a deposit of dust under it as thick as that on the floor of the rest of the room.

A curious glitter played in the flaky gold pools of the big bronze man's eyes. For a brief instant, his strange, eerie trilling sound seemed to throb through the stuffy, dead atmosphere of the room.

The dust under the box had told Doc a story, and given him a warning. The box had been placed there recently—no doubt, by Buttons—for the purpose of making a pretense at hiding the phone. That meant the call of Monk's pretty secretary had been arranged—she had been tricked into making it!

Doc Savage—expert at fathoming criminal thought processes—knew the probable explanation. He had been decoyed here. That meant there was a death trap somwhere in the abandond tenement.

Moving slowly, watching each step as though he were barefooted on a path strewn with thorns, Doc approached the room from whence came the watch ticking. He glanced in.

Lea Aster's wrist watch lay on the floor, in plain sight.

Entering with steps so hesitant and careful they were like a funeral tread, Doc circled the watch. He did not touch the watch—for he suddenly knew that to do so would mean horrible death.

It was grisly and ingenious, this death trap Buttons Zortell had set. It was a scheme which seemed impossible of failure, yet hardly that, since Doc had fathomed its secret.

Leaving the watch undisturbed, Doc conducted a rapid search of the tenement. He began at the top floor. His ransacking was barren of results until he came to a ground-floor room directly opposite the one which held the telephone. This was windowless, and had apparently been a kitchen.

A number of window sashes were stacked here. Doc had found such sashes in other rooms. Windows had been removed from the building and stacked, preparatory to being taken away by whatever salvage company had bought them.

Only one sash in the kitchen aroused Doc's interest. It, of all the collection, was wiped free of dust. Noting this, this bronze man scrutinized it closely.

Then he observed that the dust on the kitchen floor had been scuffed up considerably.

Doc carried the dustless sash to the street, placing it carefully against the curb.

He reëntered the deserted tenement, and strode to the room which held the watch. He did not touch the timepiece. From an inner pocket, he drew a small object—a common firecracker of the dime-a-package variety. This was capable of making a report like a gun-shot. It was fitted with an extra long fuse. Doc sometimes found it convenient to have a shot sound occur at one point while he was at another. He carried the firecrackers for this purpose.

He placed it carefully beside the watch, lighted it, and quit the tenement.

Picking the sash of glass from its resting place on the curb, he ran down the street, carrying it as though it were very precious.

Behind him, the earth seemed to fly to pieces. The pavement convulsed under the concussion of a terrific explosion. Smoke and débris spouted from the sashless tenement windows. Bricks fell out of the walls. Should any one have been in the vacant building, there was no question but that they would have died.

Chapter IX

ARIZONA TRAIL

Doc protected his glass sash from flying fragments by holding it partially under his coat. Plaster dust rolled into the street and surrounded him with a choking gray fog.

Monk and the others charged into view. Monk's homely face became starkly woebegone as he discovered Lea Aster was not with Doc.

"What did you find, Doc?"

"There was nobody in the place."

"But what caused that explosion?"

"I left a firecracker behind."

Monk snorted. "No firecracker could make a blast like that!"

"It didn't," Doc explained. "It merely moved your secretary's wrist watch, which was lying on the floor. Two small wires, almost too fine for the eye to see, were connected to the watch, and were broken when it was moved. Breaking them exploded a bomb in the basement."

"Then it was a trap!" Monk groaned.

"Right."

The men stared curiously at the pane of glass which Doc

was handling with such care, wondering of what importance it could be. The bronze man gave them no time for questioning. He hurried along the street until he encountered a cruising taxi.

En route to his skyscraper headquarters, he explained a little further about what he had found in the deserted tenement.

"Buttons and his gang fled, taking the girl, probably within a few moments after they tricked her into giving us the decoying phone call," he finished.

Reaching his office, Doc placed the glass pane on the inlaid table, then entered the laboratory.

He returned with a device not unlike a large edition of a box camera.

Monk looked at this mechanism, then at the glass.

"Oh-oh!" he ejaculated. "I catch on!"

Doc drew the shades, producing gloom in the office. He plugged a flexible cord which ran from the camera-like box into an electric outlet. He pointed the dark glass "eye" of the apparatus at the window sash.

A startling thing happened.

Upon the glass, where nothing had been before, there suddenly appeared, uncannily, glowing blue letters. It was as though some fantastic magic had operated.

To Doc's men, the phenomenon was an old one. They knew the explanation. The camera-like box projected invisible ultra-violet rays. Under these rays, many substances glow, or fluoresce. Capitalizing upon this latter quality, Doc had perfected a chalk which left no writing visible to the naked eye, but which sprang out in this vivid blue under the ultra-violet beam.

Each of Doc's men carried this chalk for use in penning secret messages. Although it worked most effectively on glass, it could also be used to write on practically any smooth surface. The chalk itself could be readily concealed.

Doc had even manufactured a hard variety of the strange crayon which could be made into efficient buttons.

No doubt it was with such a button that Monk's secretary had written the message upon the glass.

GATHERING close, Doc and his men translated the communication. It had been written in haste, but was perfectly legible. Lea Aster was an excellent penwoman.

It read:

I hope you find this message, Mr. Savage. Here is what I have overheard:

My captors are working under a leader in Arizona. They have a secret hide-out in Red Skull Canyon, in Arizona. This place, marked by four lights at night, is situated some miles downstream from the skull-like formation of red rock from which the canyon gets its name. I heard them telling Whitey, one of their number, where the place is. Whitey evidently intends to fly them there. They have negotiated for the purchase of a plane at the Star airport.

I heard the Mountain Desert Construction Co. mentioned, as well as the names of three men, Nate Raff, Richard O'Melia, and Ossip Keller. I could not make out what was being said, except that some peril threatens one or more of these three men. But the documents I filched——

THE script ended with that. Doc turned off the ultra-violet lantern and the pane of glass instantly became blank.

"I move we vote my secretary a medal!" Monk grinned. "She's given us a line on the secret hide-out of the gang!"

"Further than that, she has proved the connection between the Mountain Desert concern and our enemies," Doc added.

Monk's elation was only temporary. He sank again into the depths of gloom. So marked was his concern that Ham dared not make any of his usual biting remarks, something that rarely occurred. When Ham laid off Monk, it was an event.

"How are we gonna find the girl?" Monk demanded mournfully. His furry fists knotted and unknotted. His eyes roved the office, as if reluctant to remain focused for long on any one object. His gaze fixed absently on the window.

ATOP the skyscraper from which Doc's office could be seen, Buttons Zortell ducked hastily from the nickel-in-a-slot telescope through which he had been peering. He made the move instinctively, before he realized he was too far distant to be discovered.

Buttons, not daring to remain in the vicinity of the tenement where he had planted the bomb, had come to the skyscraper observation tower. He was disgusted beyond measure that Doc and the others had appeared. Uneasiness had settled upon him too.

"Blazes!" he groaned. "How'd that bomb miss gettin' them rannies!"

"Maybe a packrat tried to carry off the wrist watch and fired the nitro," suggested one of Buttons's men, who had accompanied him.

"I don't think they have packrats in this neck of the

woods," Buttons grunted. "Don't make no difference how it happened, anyhow. We fell down on the job."

"The boss ain't gonna like this."

"What about me—d'you think I'm happy?" Buttons snapped angrily. "We done our best, didn't we?"

The other changed the subject. He always became a little afraid of Buttons when the man flew into a rage. Buttons was known to have killed more than once while angry.

"What was Savage lookin' at on that hunk of glass?"

"Search me," Buttons grumbled, his wrath subsiding somewhat. "That's kinda worryin' me. This ain't an ordinary spread of gents we're up against. I'm beginnin' to think the stuff the newspapers told me about Doc Savage wasn't so much hooey as I thought."

"The boss said to clear outa town if the bombin' failed," his hireling reminded.

"Don't think we ain't gonna do it, either!" Buttons grunted. "Back in them Red Skull brakes, I'll stake myself against any fightin' men! Here in the city, I ain't so sure of myself."

"What about the girl?"

"We'll take her along—of course."

The pair hurried down a winding staircase to the elevator landing.

MONK had observed nothing of the little tableau on the distant skyscraper observation tower. He moved his tired gaze to his companions.

"I wonder what can be back of all this," he ruminated. "From the ending of my secretary's message, I believe she had just started to tell us what was in the documents she lifted from Buttons. She must have been interrupted."

Doc Savage was thumbing through a telephone directory, and did not look up.

"What are you hunting, Doc?" Ham asked.

"Miss Aster mentioned that the gang had purchased a plane at the Star airport," Doc told him.

"Huh!" Monk exploded. "I overlooked that angle!"

Doc found the flying field number and put in a call. He got no answer. A second try a few moments later was also fruitless.

"The drome isn't far out," he declared. "We'll drive."

Doc kept a number of automobiles in a special garage in the basement of the gigantic building. Outside of the skyscraper employees, very few persons knew of the existence of this garage. A large elevator lifted the machines to the street.

Doc selected a touring car of moderate size and plain color, a machine that was inconspicuous. Although presenting no quality out of the ordinary to a casual observer, the chassis of the vehicle possessed unusual strength, and the engine developed in excess of two hundred horsepower.

The machine whisked them through traffic, over one of the bridges which give access to Manhattan, and out a busy boulevard. Within less than half an hour, Doc guided the car upon the tarmac of the Star airport.

A small drome, it apparently did little business. A few rusty metal hangars and a ramshackle board office comprised the equipment.

No one was in sight.

But in the shack of an office, they found an unconscious man. He had been felled by a blow upon the temple. It took Doc ten minutes to revive him and obtain his story.

"I'm the manager," the man mumbled, still dazed. "Yeah, I sold some guys a plane—an eight-passenger, single-motored green metal monoplane."

"Who struck you?"

"The guys I sold the ship to. They showed up about twenty minutes ago. They was draggin' a girl with 'em. She was a blonde, a peach! It looked like she was in trouble, and I started to interfere. One of the guys popped me on the head with a six-shooter as big as a cannon."

Doc and his men exchanged glances.

"They took off with Lea Aster, it's certain," Monk muttered. "I'm bettin' they're headed for Arizona!"

"Come!" Doc clipped. He made swiftly for the touring car. The engine started moaning the instant he was under the wheel. The others piled in as the machine whipped into motion.

"I reckon we're bound for Arizona, huh?" Monk questioned hopefully.

"You said it!" Doc told him grimly.

Chapter X

MAN BATS

SOME sixteen hours later, a lonely sheep-herder in the rugged mesa and canyon country of Arizona was witness to something which he did not soon forget.

This shepherd had bedded his flock for the night on a shelflike bit of ground near the crest of a gently sloping butte. He was sitting up with a shotgun in hopes of getting a crack at a pair of coyotes which had been molesting his sheep.

Suddenly there came to the sheep-herder's ears a shrill hissing. The noise mounted with startling abruptness until it was a tremendous scream.

Over the mesa top flashed a monster apparition. It blackened the stars. It seemed to travel with the speed of light, for it was quickly gone, leaving behind a dying whistle, not unlike the sound of a motor siren running down. The shepherd saw only that the thing had a shape vaguely resembling a legless, headless bat of a distinctive bronze color.

The sheep-herder was astounded, puzzled; for no motor roar had accompanied the fast-flying night phantom. If the thing was a plane, it was one of unusual type, and traveling at least two hundred and fifty miles an hour.

The night monster was just that—a plane of remarkable design. It was Doc Savage's speed ship. The extremeness of its streamlining marked the craft from others. Three great motors were contained entirely within wings and fuselage. The landing gear, even the tail skid, disappeared so as to offer no wind resistance.

Doc and his five aides rode in the fore part of the cabin. They were somewhat crowded for room. The cabin was spacious, but at the moment filled with a bulky cargo A brownish cloth covered the load.

The three motors were fitted with efficient silencers, and the propellers were of a radical design which reduced the customary air scream. Traveling at reduced speed, the plane was practically noiseless. At full throttle, it made only a shrill hissing sound.

The cabin was built like a vacuum bottle, airtight and noiseproof. Conversation could proceed in ordinary tones.

"We're about eighty miles from Red Skull Canyon," Renny offered, looking up from a pad on which he had been figuring their location.

Renny was navigating. His engineering knowledge fitted him for the job.

Doc himself handled the controls.

Long Tom, the somewhat unhealthy-looking electrical wizard, was working with the powerful radio equipment—in touch with airport stations along their back trail. Now he turned away from the loudspeaker—headphones were unnecessary in the silenced cabin.

"No luck," he reported. "A plane answering the description of the green, all-metal crate carrying Buttons and his gang, took on gas at an airport near Kirksville, Missouri. The girl was along. The airport attendant had the description we broadcast, and he sent for the sheriff. But the gang got away before the officer arrived. They haven't been seen since."

"We should be at least four hours ahead of them," Doc decided. "This ship is much faster than theirs."

Monk had been peering downward.

"Whew!" he grunted over a sloping shoulder. "This country we're gettin' over looks like a pilot's nightmare!"

GRAY clouds were bunched in the night sky. The moonlight crowned them with beautiful silver, but underneath they were black and ominous. The moving moon shadows cast by the clouds showed they were being swept along at a rapid clip by high air currents.

Penetrating through breaks in the clouds like searchlight beams, the luminance from the moon disclosed flat-topped mesas, slopes shaggy with mesquite and sage and cactus, gulches that might have been gouged by a gigantic knife, and canyons which seemed yawning and bottomless cracks.

Doc decreased the engine speed.

"We'll land around here somewhere," he said.

He moved a lever, causing vanishing flaps to appear on the plane wing. These enabled the craft to cruise at very low speed without loss of altitude. Another lever lowered the landing gear.

Doc selected the tablelike top of a mesa, circled twice, and dropped the plane in for a landing. The ship leaped wildly as it hit a sage clump. The wheels struck a growth of jumping cactus, causing thorny fragments to shower high in the air. Wheel brakes pulled the ship to a stop.

"We're now about fifteen miles from Red Skull Canyon," Renny announced.

No more was said. The men knew the task ahead. They went to work with silent efficiency.

The brownish cloth was pulled off the cargo. Unfolded, the piece of fabric proved to be of considerable size. It was streaked in lighter hues, to imitate the veining in rock. Spread over the plane, it could be used to camouflage the craft as a large boulder.

Latches were operated, permitting one whole side of the plane cabin to hinge outward. This formed an inclined runway to the baked mesa top. Down it, the men rolled the bulky article of cargo.

This contrivance resembled the fuselage of a small, stubby airplane. But the tail, instead of having elevators and rudder, was fitted with rudder alone. The undercarriage had four doughnut-like wheels, mounted caster fashion to permit the craft to roll in any direction.

Above the fuselage projected a streamlined hump, perhaps four feet in height, and tapering to a tublike cluster of sockets and connecting rods. From the cabin of the huge speed ship came vane-shaped wings, which were secured in the sockets. The outer tips of these were equipped with what resembled miniature elevators and rudders.

Into this unique craft, Doc placed parachutes and several compact boxes of apparatus. He and Renny occupied the tiny two-seated cockpit.

A strong, chemically-cooled motor started within the vehicle. The vane-like wings began to revolve, windmill fashion. They increased speed.

The ship lifted straight off the ground. It was a true gyroplane, of Doc's own development. Like the more prosaic autogyro, it was not capable of tremendous speed.

Manipulating the controls, Doc sent the gyro northward. The controls consisted, in addition to the usual throttle and navigation instruments, of an auto type wheel mounted on a rocker arm. Turning the wheel steered the ship; pulling it back caused a climb, and shoving it forward produced descent.

The gyro was a perfect craft for service over the tortured land that lay below.

ANGRY wind currents, glancing up the sides of buttes and boiling out of abysmal canyons, caused the gyro to toss about. The motor was well muffled, and the spinning wings made only a faint moan.

The better to survey the terrain below, Doc donned light, high-magnification binoculars mounted in a spectacle frame. These closely resembled the conventional "sportocular."

"There's the valley which will be flooded by the dam!" Renny exclaimed suddenly.

Although their departure from New York had been sudden, Doc and his men had been able to learn something of the dam being built by the Mountain Desert Construction Company. A trade journal had supplied their information.

The valley to be flooded was several miles wide and a number of times as long. Ages ago, it had no doubt formed the bed of a vast natural lake, hemmed in by mountainous country. The waters had drained away, cutting a deep channel through a range of the mountains. The channel, a sheer-walled gash, was Red Skull Canyon.

The dam, across the entrance of the canyon, was intended to turn the valley into a miniature replica of the great lake it had once been. Electricity generated at the dam was to be sold to cities and industrial plants in Arizona, California, and other states.

Doc turned his aërial vehicle toward the canyon mouth. Moving patches of moonlight furnished faint illumination. Cliffs shoved up walls of solid stone, dark, forbidding. Here and there were detached formations resembling giant cathedral spires.

The entrance of Red Skull Canyon yawned a great mouth. In the bottom of this draped strings of electric lights. Work was evidently proceeding day and night. Clouds of dust rolled like steam in the glare of electric bulbs. Red Skull River, held back by coffer dams and diverted through tunnels, was remindful of a fat brown snake.

"The dam is not far from completion!" declared Renny, who had himself superintended the building of not a few such structures. "They're running the final concrete."

Doc now pulled the gyro up into a cloud. He had swung to the northward for a reason—wind was carrying the clouds south. Without trouble, he kept the craft within the vapor. He dropped down from time to time to have a look at what was beneath.

They passed over the busy dam scene. The canyon gaped below. It was a crevasse in stone, of tremendous depth. Moonbeams, penetrating rifts in the clouds, slanted far into it, as if striving to reach the thundering river that was its life blood, but the bottom remained in darkness.

Doc descended more often below the concealing cloud. His eyes roved intently, seeking something to indicate the lair of his enemies.

"There is the rock formation from which the canyon and river were named," he told Renny at one point of the flight.

Staring, Renny saw it distinctly. Rounded, hideous, a great knob of stone jutted up beside the canyon. This had a striking likeness to a huge human skull. Its color was pale, unwholesome, contrasting to the darker hue of the surroundings. It seemed a foreboding sign of danger and death.

The gyro floated on. Miles dropped behind.

"There we are!" Doc clipped.

His sharp eyes had picked out four pin points of light. They formed a long, narrow rectangle.

At a height of nearly a mile, hugging the blackness of the cloud, Doc guided his craft into position above the lights. He donned a parachute, after surrendering the controls to Renny.

About his middle, he strapped a wide belt. A number of rather bulky, padded boxes were already affixed to this.

There was no dramatic leave-taking, although both knew Doc faced deadly peril. The leap alone held incalculable danger, since a man dropping by parachute has a limited choice of landings.

"Go back to the others and wait for orders," Doc commanded.

Then he stepped overboard.

AIR screamed past his ears as he fell. He began to turn slowly over and over, but an expert forward fling of both legs stopped that. The monster rent of a canyon seemed to leap apart like giant jaws and swallow him. Even then, he did not tug the chute ripcord. He did not want air currents to toss him about and perhaps carry him wide of his mark.

Darkness increased. Below, the four lights spread, as though carried by an invisible hand.

They evidently marked the limits of a landing field.

At one end, a faint glow appeared—reflection of a camp fire upon rock.

The instant he saw this reddish beach, Doc cracked his 'chute. It opened with a yank which might have seriously damaged an individual less muscular than Doc.

Grasping the shrouds on one side, he slipped the 'chute away from the bilious glow. In the black abyss, he could judge his nearness to the ground only by position of the marker lights. He kept his leg muscles tense for the shock.

It came a bit sooner than he expected. He was able to keep his feet. Running with the 'chute, he emptied it of air. Crouching on the folds, he shucked off the harness.

He listened. There was no alarm. Evidently the men here did not expect a visit from the air. The firelight, he saw now, was at least a hundred feet above the level of the field. It shone out of a square opening on the sheer side of a cliff!

Doc bundled the parachute. Stepping cautiously, for a cloud had blocked out the moon face and the gloom was intense, Doc moved to one side. Sandy earth lay underfoot, indicating this was a shelf well up from the canyon bottom— possibly at one time it had been the river bed.

He encountered a gulch some distance beyond the rectangle inclosed by the lights. He descended to the bottom and crept down it until his way was blocked by a sheer drop of—a pebble tossed over gave the depth—at least a hundred feet.

From one of the belt pouches, he removed various tubes and bottles. He worked with the aid of a hooded flashlight, washing his face and hands with a chemical which gave his skin a pale, unhealthy cast. A dye darkened his hair. A chemical cleanser could remove this make-up.

He concealed parachute and pack belt in a crack in the rock, covering them with boulders. Then he returned to the level ground. Silently, he approached the glow on the cliff, only to be surprised by the discovery that the rock rose sheer and unscalable.

He purposefully made a little noise.

A revolver instantly roared from above. With a loud, vicious thud, a bullet planted itself in the sand at his feet.

Chapter XI

THE CANYON FIGHT

Doc did not change position. The gunman could not see him, anyway. Giving his voice a brutal coarseness and a tearing note of rage, he sent a shout upward.

"What d'you think this is, anyhow!"

"It ain't no place to go strollin' in the dark!" came the snarled retort. "Who're you, hombre?"

"I'm the jasper that's gonna walk your carcass if you throw any more lead!" Doc bellowed, simulating the truculent manner of one tough guy addressing another.

"How many men are with you?"

"I don't need any help to take care of you!" Doc blustered up at the gunman.

"Cut the clownin'! Did the boss come with you?"

"No!" said Doc, taking advantage of this tip that the master mind was not present. "I'm gonna wait here for 'im."

"Don't be too sure of that! Are you the sheriff?"

"Are you tryin' to insult me?" Doc howled.

Laughter rattled from the man overhead. He seemed to consider the sheriff query a great joke.

"Hang around," he directed. "I'm comin' down to interview you, sweetheart!"

Instead of one man, several descended a rope ladder which they flung down the cliff face. They brought electric lanterns.

The Arizona penitentiary and all the dives on the border could have been combed without netting a more savage-looking collection. A slovenly beard stubble decorated most of the faces. They all would have benefited from a bath.

The man who had shot at Doc, a tubby individual with ears thickened and nose flattened as the result of much pounding, scowled darkly.

"So the boss sent you here to wait for 'im, huh?"

"You don't think I'm here for my health do you?" Doc snorted. He was deliberately assuming the character of a hard-boiled personage. With insolent, flippant answers, he could evade dangerous questions.

"Your health is gonna be affected if you keep on crackin' wise!" grated the other. "I never saw you before."

"That's your loss."

"Oh, yeah? Are you a new man?"

"You might call me that."

The stocky man glanced about meaningly at his companions. "This guy showin' up looks kinda fishy to me. The boss ain't said nothin' about takin' on any new hands."

"Does the boss have to ask your permission?" Doc growled sarcastically.

"What trail did you use comin' here?" the fellow countered.

"Don't make me laugh!" Doc snorted—and hoped mightily that some hint would show him the proper answer.

Two of the other men laughed.

"You can't kid this fellow, Jud!" one told the burly man. "He knows the only way of reachin' this place alive is by water—an' plane."

The remark was illuminating. The men must have a power boat on Red Skull River, a craft able to cope with the current.

"Who brought you up?" the tubby Jud persisted.

Doc bent a fierce glare upon his questioner.

"Maybe you have to have somebody lead you up that river," he sneered, "but I don't!"

"Oh!" Jud looked vastly enlightened. "So the boss took you on because you know this country an' the river?"

Doc, ignoring the remark, waved an arm overhead. "You hombres know the plane from New York is comin' in before long, don't you?"

"Sure."

"And you know about the girl?"

"Sure. We got a radio up above. The boss slips us important orders over that."

The remark about the wireless set was bad news to Doc. Suppose these men should get in touch with their leader in an effort to verify his connection with the gang? This would disrupt his careful plans.

"I'm here to take charge of the girl!" he continued.

The men showed no surprise at the remark. One greeted it with a rowdy snort.

"What's the matter? Ain't we good enough to keep the city dame company?"

Doc decided to put in a few words which they might later recall as a warning.

"The man that harms that girl signs his own death warrang!" he growled vehemently. "And don't any of you hombres forget that! She may be the price that will buy Doc Savage off, in case he gets us cornered. If she is harmed in the slightest, it's gonna be just too bad!"

For a moment, Doc thought he might have put the speech a bit too forcibly. The group gave him curious stares. But the incident was permitted to pass.

Doc was invited to mount the rope ladder which hung down the vertical cliff face. He did so. It led him into the square opening which he had first glimpsed from the air.

Beyond the aperture was a stone room, in the center of which a camp fire burned fitfully. Doc gazed about, not a little surprised. Other rooms opened off this one, and still more seemed to form additional stories. The walls were of roughly shaped stone, set in a dry-mud mortar. Stout timbers supported the ceiling and the floors above.

It was an ancient cliff dwelling—a ruin of the type not at all uncommon in Arizona and other Southwestern States.

Built hundreds, possibly thousands of years ago, by some race long forgotten, the structure was in good preservation. Outlines of human fingers could be seen upon the mortar. The dry climate had kept the wooden timbers from decaying.

"A nifty hang-out, eh?" suggested one of the men.

"It is—if it don't fall down on you!" Doc retorted gruffly.

"It won't—not after standin' this long. I'll bet nobody had been in it for a thousand years, until the boss found it. He said he had a dickens of a time gettin' up to it."

Doc, standing well out of the firelight, began to fish slyly for information.

"When did he find it?" he asked, feigning only cursory interest.

"I dunno. Before the dam buildin' started, I guess."

"How come the boss to be pokin' around this region?"

The other man looked surprised. "You don't know much about the boss, do you?"

"No."

"How'd you come to tie up with him?"

"Through a friend of his—Buttons." And that, Doc reflected, was no lie!

"Buttons Zortell, eh?" said the other, making conversation.

"Buttons is quite a guy, but I hear he didn't do so well in New York."

"Who cares about Buttons!" Doc yawned. "What I'm interested in, partner, is learnin' more about this scatter I'm mixed up in. The boss didn't have time to tell me much. What's the kitty in this thing? What're we after?"

Doc was alert for the slightest sign of hostility after he put the bold query. He expected such ignorance in an accepted member of the gang to arouse instant suspicion. But he got a surprise.

The men emitted snorts of laughter.

"We don't know ourselves what the big boss is after!" one chuckled. "We get paid; we do our work; we keep our mouths shut. That's all there is to it."

"It must be somethin' in connection with the dam!" Doc suggested.

"With keepin' the dam from gettin' built, you mean!"

Doc filed this bit of news for future consideration. So there was opposition to the building of the dam!

"I see!" he grunted. "But what about the boss? What little I know, I got through Buttons."

The other man seemed unsuspicious. "What d'you want me to tell you?"

Doc reflected silently that almost anything would be of interest.

"His name is supposed to be a big secret, huh?" he asked.

A puzzled squint puckered the eyes of the man before him. "I don't quite savvy what you're drivin' at. Of course it's a secret outside the gang. But everybody in the gang knows 'is name ain't Nick Clipton."

"Hey—you!" suddenly roared squat Jud, who had first discovered Doc.

The fellow had moved around to the side and surreptitiously drawn a six-gun. He had the weapon leveled at Doc's head.

"You ain't one of this scatter, atall!" snarled the gunman.

Doc hastily assumed his hard-boiled, domineering character.

"You're fixin' to get yourself ventilated, hombre!" he rasped.

Jud's big single-action revolver jutted forward threateningly.

"I'm wise to you!" he spat. "There was somethin' phony about you right from taw!"

"Smart boy!"

"You're durn tootin' I am! I'll prove it, too! If you're on

the up-and-up, you can give us the real name of the boss.
What is it?"

Doc would have given a lot to be able to supply the cor-
rect answer to that question. Not because he was greatly
concerned over his dangerous position—he had stood before
killer guns on other occasions. But the main purpose behind
his talk with these men had been to learn the name of the
master mind who paid them.

"The only name I know him by is Nick Clipton," he
growled—truthfully.

The men exchanged alarmed glances. Then they all drew
guns.

"By golly, I believe you're right about 'im!" one told Jud.

"Sure I'm right!"

"You dumb sheep-herders!" Doc roared. "I know how we
can settle this! Call the boss on the radio an' ask him about
me!"

The suggestion was not bluff on his part. He wanted them
to call—and as they called, he hoped to overhear the name
of their leader.

But they saw through his subterfuge.

"Nix!" grinned Jud derisively. "That radio is an old spark-
coil set that can be heard all over the joint when it's goin'.
You could hear the boss's name. We'll just tie you up an'
decide what to do later."

They advanced threateningly, guns ready.

A close observer might have seen Doc's chest expand, as
though he were drawing a capacity quantity of air, and
holding it within his lungs. His hands were above his head
—yet for no apparent reason, the biceps of his right arm
tensed and swelled until it stretched the sleeve of his coat.

The foremost man reached out to search him. A weird
thing happened. The reaching effort seemed to overcome the
man. He fell, limp as a rag, flat on his face.

An instant later, the other gunmen toppled over in the
same uncanny fashion. They lay where they fell, breathing
noisily. Every man was unconscious.

Doc Savage waited a bit longer than a minute, then released the breath he had been holding. Retaining his breath
over that interval was, for Doc, no great effort.

Inside his right coat sleeve, over the biceps, was a small,
secret pocket. This had held several thin-walled glass balls.
They contained a quick-spreading anæsthetic gas which produced instant unconsciousness—yet which became harmless
after diffused in the air more than a minute.

Doc had merely broken the balls to release the gas, by tensing his tremendous biceps muscle, and held his breath until the vapor became impotent. The men would be senseless for some time.

As he stood there drawing in lungfuls of the dry night air, a plane came moaning down into the abyss of Red Skull Canyon. Exhaust sound indicated it was a single-motored ship.

Buttons Zortell was to come in such a craft! Doc flung to the rectangle of an opening. His eyes probed the darkness.

Clouds had momentarily parted above the mighty rent in the earth, letting down chalky moonlight which whitened the rock spires and canyon rim, but left the depths in gloom. Echoes of the plane motor bounced in salvos from the beetling cliffs, making it seem that a thousand aircraft labored in the chasm.

Wing-tip lights, blinking off and on in signal, betrayed the location of the ship. It was circling in the moonlight, keeping directly above the four ground lights.

Doc knew there must be an arrangement to illuminate the field. With his small flashlight, he made a quick search. An adjoining room of the cliff dwelling, also looking out upon the level terrain below, held the lighting device.

It was an ordinary washtub, aimed like a searchlight at the ground, and fitted with a friction-igniting flare.

Doc hastily tore off the friction end of the flare and scraped it aflame. The brilliance which resulted was blinding. Details of the landing field were disclosed.

It was his first opportunity for a comprehensive survey, and Doc delayed a moment to take in the scene.

The shelf of ground, several acres in area, was even smoother than he expected. Located at the point where a large side canyon joined Red Skull, the shelf was open in three directions—at least open enough to enable an expert pilot to make a landing. The fourth side was walled by the cliff.

Doc hurried to the rope ladder and started down. He could not make out details of the plane, as yet. It had not come within the flare luminance.

The rope ladder swayed as Doc descended, scraping along the vertical stone. Below was a sheer drop of at least a hundred feet. Above, there was no way of telling how high the abrupt stone lifted.

Doc had covered but a few feet when the ladder gave a sharp, inexplicable jerk. An instant later, it collapsed completely.

It had been cut at the top!

Chapter XII

KILLER CHASM

Doc had not been unwarned. The first jerk of the ladder had indicated severing of the rope strands on one side.

He reached swiftly for the nearest ledge. This was little more than a roughness, barely offering purchase for Doc's grasping fingers. But it sufficed, and he was dangling from it at the moment the ladder failed.

Overhead, a man swore delightedly.

The voice was a new one to Doc. Evidently this man had come from within the cliff dwelling somewhere. Perhaps he had been suspicious from the first, and kept in the background where the gas had not reached him.

Clinging by the grip of one hand, Doc produced a hank of stout silken line from within his clothing. To one end of this was secured a collapsible metal grapple hook.

Doc anchored the grapple, tested it, then slid down the cord, maintaining control over his progress by keeping a turn of the line about his leg. Once he had reached the bottom, a flip of the cord freed the grapple.

A gun crashed overhead. The bullet jarred dust out of the ground near Doc's feet.

The cliff had a slight bulge. He flattened close to the base, making it necessary for the man above to lean far over to shoot.

The plane was coming in for a landing, motor echoes making a bawling, like a multitude of lions.

Doc flung a glance at the craft—and got a profound surprise.

This was no green monoplane, such as Buttons Zortell had purchased in New York! It was a yellow ship, a cabin biplane.

A six-gun slug smacked unpleasantly close to Doc, and he hastily shifted position. The man above was yelling angrily. Forced to lean far out to see his target, he could not shoot accurately. Moreover, the flare did not cast a lot of light at the cliff base.

Doc selected two round rocks slightly smaller than baseballs. Creeping back and forth to baffle the gunner above, he waited and watched the plane.

The craft flattened, settled slowly. Dust arose as its wheels touched. It braked to a halt. The propeller came to a jerky standstill.

The instant the prop stopped, Doc sprang out a few yards from the cliff, calculated accurately, and flung both his round rocks upward.

Both dornicks hit his target—the flare. With a shower of white-hot sparks, the inflammable portion was knocked out of the tub of a reflector. This fell the hundred feet to the foot of the cliff, and was extinguished by the impact.

Doc Savage, now enwrapped in darkness, sprinted for the plane. He wanted to reach it before the motor could be started and the craft turned for a take-off.

He had no idea who the men in the plane were, but that question was answered in short order.

"Boss!" screeched the man in the cliff dwelling. "Watch out!"

A MOMENT after crying the warning, the man succeeded in igniting another flare, and fixing it in the reflector.

With the squirt of light across the shelf, Doc cast his gaze at the plane, hoping to glimpse the features of the master mind. That the brains of the gang had arrived in the ship, the yell of the man on the cliff had clearly disclosed.

Four men occupied the plane cabin. But to Doc's disappointment, they had yanked down wide-brimmed hats and were holding handkerchiefs before their faces, hiding their identity. They drew revolvers and began firing at Doc Savage.

Gone were all Doc's chances of reaching the plane. He twisted aside and sped for the small gully where he had left his parachute and pack belt. This offered the nearest shelter.

Bullets stormed his course. The men in the plane were fair marksmen. The flare blazing in their eyes handicapped them, however. Before they accustomed themselves to the glare, Doc had dived into the gulch.

Leaping from the plane, still keeping their faces concealed, the men prepared to charge recklessly after Doc. But a shrieked warning came from the fellow in the cliff dwelling.

"Be careful!" he cried. "That hombre must be Doc Savage!"

The gang at the plane glanced to one of their number for orders.

This man—obviously the master villain of the organization—was muffled from neck to toes in a light gabardine coat. He had tied a colored bandanna in front of his features.

His gray cowboy hat was hauled low. There was nothing distinctive about his size.

"Get that guy!" gritted the master mind, waving an arm at the spot where Doc had disappeared. "I don't give a whoop who he is! Get 'im!"

They charged the gully rim, six-guns at cock, eyes straining until they ached.

The men did not expect Doc to present himself at the exact point where he had vanished, but that was what happened. Doc bobbed up in a way that seemed magic. His arm flashed forward in a throwing motion. He was out of sight again so swiftly that a volley of lead fired at him did nothing but spade up showers of dust and sand.

The object he had thrown broke with a small tinkling noise, only a few yards in front of the charging group.

"Watch out for gas!" screeched the man in the cliff ruin.

The runners heeded the warning instantly. They did not even delay to ascertain exactly what Doc had flung. They veered off, sprinting madly.

Their course took them away from the plane and toward the cliff. Momentarily, they expected to be gassed. The fellow in the ruin added to their fear by bellowing news of what had happened to his companions. At the same time, he threw down another rope ladder—one evidently kept for emergencies. The men from the plane clambered up this in a frenzy of anxiety.

Doc Savage watched them with mingled feelings. By the light of the flare, he could distinguish the object, the throwing of which had produced such terror. It lay near a flat rock it had struck in landing—but it hardly looked dangerous.

It was Doc's watch!

THINGS were now in a state of mutual checkmate. Doc could not quit the gully—he found it ended in a sheer drop to the boiling, muddy river. His enemies, not knowing they had been deceived by nothing more frightful than a watch, dared not leave their lofty perch. But they sent bullets ripping across the gulch.

Doc kept a close watch on the cliff dwelling. He saw the gabardine-coated man he knew to be the master mind, but could pick out nothing which might later identify the fellow.

The flare burned away. Another was lighted.

Something like twenty minutes dragged past. Far off in the night, the roaring moan of a plane engine materialized.

Doc immediately went into action. From his pack belt, he produced a tiny radio transmitter and receiver. An insulated metal tape flung along the gully bottom furnished all the aërial necessary.

Once the set was in operation, he sent briskly for two or three minutes.

In the meantime, the approaching plane had dropped down into the canyon in a series of tight turns. It came finally within the zone whitened by the powerful flare.

An eight-place, single-motored green metal monoplane! It answered the description of the craft purchased by Buttons Zortell in New York.

The pilot was evidently suspicious, since he circled the field steadily instead of making a move to land.

In one of the windowlike apertures in the cliff dwelling wall, the man in the gabardine coat appeared. He flailed both arms, gesticulating for Buttons Zortell to attack the gully which harbored Doc.

For once, Doc could have made good use of a gun. No firearm was at hand, however. He never carried one, although he could handle them with unbelievable accuracy.

There was a good psychological reason behind Doc's decision not to carry a gun—he did not want to form the habit of relying on one, for well did he know that no person is quite as much at loss as a gunman without his gun.

Those in the plane comprehended the orders of their boss. The ship promptly dived upon Doc's gully. Rifles and pistols lipped flame from the cabin windows.

Doc haunted shadows in the bottom of the wash and escaped damage. But he was not to triumph so easily! The attacking plane climbed upward a few hundred feet and those aboard tossed out a parachute flare. This light whitened the gulch bottom, disclosing Doc.

Eagerly, the men swept back to the attack. For a moment, the sheer walls of the gulch concealed their quarry.

In the few seconds that he was hidden from them, Doc flung to the floor of the wash and swiftly covered himself with sand.

The monoplane thundered over the gully. The men aboard had their guns ready. But they let fly nothing but profanity. They were unable to distinguish the sandy mound which concealed Doc. They knew what he must have done, but the light was not sufficiently brilliant to disclose him.

The green craft circled aimlessly while those aboard debated ways and means.

Doc watched the heavens expectantly. He was not surprised when two planes plunged suddenly into the flare-whitened canyon. One was his giant speed ship, the other his gyroplane—they had not lost much time in answering his radio summons.

BUTTONS ZORTELL and his pilot, Whitey, abandoned the attack the instant they discovered the new arrivals. The green monoplane climbed madly in an effort to escape.

It was overhauled quickly by Doc's monster speed ship— the big bus was capable of a top speed at least twice that of its quarry. Along the leading edge of the wings, there suddenly appeared a series of gory red tongues. These were flaming machine-gun muzzles, the weapons themselves being built within the wing.

Tracer bullets streaked gray and red about the green monoplane. The craft seemed stitched around with ghastly threads. Yet no bullets touched the metal ship, for blonde Lea Aster was aboard.

The green bus whipped into a mad dive. Her crew had realized they could never escape by air. They headed for the flare-lighted bench of ground below them.

Whitey made a hasty and very bad landing. His craft bounced, careened, but kept upright. It halted near the cliff. The scared passengers piled out—six sweating men and one defiant but helpless blonde girl.

Catching sight of Monk's secretary, Doc popped from the gulch. But a rain of bullets, fired from the cliff ruin, drove him back.

Buttons Zortell ran up the rope ladder to safety. Whitey followed, then the others. Lea Aster refused to climb—so they tied her to the lower end of the ladder and pulled her up after the last man had ascended.

Renny, flying the gyro, now dropped down to take Doc aboard. This maneuver, was covered by machine-gun fire from the speed plane.

"I believe we have the entire gang cornered!" Doc told Renny, as the gyro lifted out of gunshot of the ruin.

"Their big chief, too?" Renny demanded.

"I believe so. He arrived shortly before the plane got in from New York. And every man jack of them is now in that cliff dwelling."

"What did their leader look like?"

"Search me!" Doc retorted, then explained that he had been able to distinguish nothing because of the gabardine coat.

"Well, their goose is cooked, anyhow!" Renny boomed. "They've trapped themselves! They can't escape down the face of that cliff! And not even a fly could climb upward!"

Chapter XIII
HOT ROCK

Doc now issued low orders. Complying with them, Renny maneuvered the windmilling gyro in close to the cliff face. Pushing the control wheel forward gently, he lowered the strange craft.

From within the ruin, a man sought to shoot upward. But after releasing a single bullet, he was driven to cover by a blast of lead from the monster speed plane. The latter craft was cruising back and forth along the cliff face—no mean feat of piloting. Monk was at the controls. All of Doc's five aides were expert flyers.

The flare burning in the tin tub was extinguished. The darkness which ensued was only momentary—the speed plane dropped a 'chute flare to take its place.

There was no more shooting from within the ruins. Nor did the villains show themselves, although they must have known the gyro was nearing the rectangular openings which gave access to their stronghold. This seemed a bit strange.

When within a few yards of the first aperture, Doc flung a glass ball which was nearly as large as a grapefruit. This passed into the ancient cliff dwelling structure and burst.

It held the instantaneously effective, quick-dissipating anæsthetic gas, the exact composition of which was known to no one but Doc.

The silk cord and grapple which had served earlier in the night were now brought into use. From the fairly steady cockpit of the gyro, Doc tossed the grapple repeatedly until it hung on the edge of an opening in the ruin. Then he dropped the cord down the cliff face.

Renny promptly landed the gyro, permitting Doc to alight and climb the cord.

To a man of ordinary strength, mounting the slender line of silk might have presented an impossible task. The small size made gripping difficult. Doc's hands possessed amazing strength, thanks to an intensive system of exercises which he took each day of his life. He climbed swiftly. Not once did the cord slip through his powerful grasp.

"Hear anything?" Renny called anxiously from below.

"No," Doc replied, after listening.

Renny's sigh of relief came up distinctly. "I guess the gas got 'em!"

Some forty feet below his objective, Doc suddenly halted. His sensitive nostrils moved slightly as he sampled the air.

"What is it?" Renny asked.

"An odor—as though something were burning!" Doc explained.

"That's probably from the flares."

Doc said nothing more, but this scent he had detected did not come from the flares. Of that, he was convinced. The question of just what it was had him baffled. It had a tang new to his experience.

He slid back down and joined Renny.

"It might be some type of poison gas," he answered Renny's look of surprise. "The odor is very strange!"

Monk brought the speed plane down in a graceful landing. The big craft taxied close, and its four passengers alighted.

The cabin still held several cases and boxes. From one of these Doc dug his chemical-reaction device for ascertaining the presence of poison gas.

He also got another object—a large glass bottle which could be sealed absolutely tight.

With these slung on his back, he mounted the silk cord. No stir, no sound of life came from the ruin.

There was nothing poisonous about the strange odor, his apparatus told him. He entered the cliff dwelling.

To his surprise, there was no sign of tubby Jud or the other men who had fallen victim to the gas-in-the-coat-sleeve trick.

Doc tossed the rope ladder down to his men. They joined him, with the exception of Long Tom and Ham, who remained on watch—there was always a chance more of the villains would arrive by plane.

The strange odor became stronger as they stepped into an inner room of the ancient structure. Doc played his flash beam about. It revealed a circular hole in the floor. The end of a pole projected from this. Notches had been cut into the pole, making it a ladder of sorts.

Leaning over the hole, Doc found the weird smell much stronger. And there now seemed to be heat.

Renny, Monk, and Johnny had scattered to other rooms. They came back, puzzled.

"There's no sign of the gang!" they reported.

"They must've gone down that hole!" Monk grunted.

Doc dropped anæsthetic down the gaping aperture. He and his men gave it the necessary minute to become ineffective, then descended.

They found themselves in one of several chambers chipped out of solid stone. These were floored with the rubble of ages.

Spying another floor opening, and making sure the odor—and intense heat—was coming from it, Doc descended. The others followed.

"Holy cow!" Renny ejaculated. "Somethin' must be awful hot in there ahead of us!"

"Monk!" Doc called. He had lost sight of the hairy chemist.

"I'm just lookin' in here!" Monk informed him from another room. "These chambers seem to have been a granary! I see a lot of corn cobs around."

"Did you ever smell anything like this odor?" Doc questioned.

Monk sniffed noisily. "Bless me! No!"

"You sure? I thought perhaps you had caught such a scent while mixing chemicals."

"Never did. And, say—where'd everybody go to? And where's that heat comin' from?"

His flash beam playing ahead, Doc ducked through a low door. The heat was more intense. It increased as he advanced. A strange, reddish panel became visible ahead. This proved to be another door—with a great mass beyond it, glowing at a red heat!

Doc stopped—stared in wonder. Monk and Renny came up behind him.

"That looks like red-hot lava," Monk muttered in awe.

THEY sidled forward gingerly. The heat was terrific. It dried the moisture in their eyes, set perspiration trickling on their skin. Yet the source of the terrific temperature was fully forty feet distant, at the end of a long chamber which was half room and half passage.

The whole end of the subterranean room glowed a cherry color. In one corner, the solid stone seemed to have melted! Not unlike red cotton, the molten rock had oozed outward over an area of several square feet, pouring out into a shape that resembled a human skull!

With a quick gesture, Doc uncorked the glass flask he had brought. He fanned it about briskly until it contained a quantity of the air within the stone cubicle, then corked it.

"What's the idea?" Renny wanted to know.

"Some of the air—to analyze later," Doc explained. "This odor has me mystified."

"To me, that melted rock is a bigger mystery!" Monk muttered. "And where's my secretary? Where's everybody?"

Doc pointed at the patch of molten rock. "Don't the shape of that tell you something?"

Monk squinted.

"For cryin' out loud!" he yelled. "That's a door! And molten rock has oozed through from the other side, fillin' it!"

"Exactly."

"But what could have made heat enough to melt the rock like that?"

Doc did not answer. Instead, he rapped: "You birds look this place over! See what you can find!"

Then he was gone, vanishing with the speed and silence of a bronze apparition. A moment later, he was descending the cliff face.

Long Tom and Ham, guarding the planes, were not aware of his presence until he appeared, phantomlike, beside them.

"Heard anything?" he asked them.

"A minute ago!" Ham admitted. "I thought I heard a motor. But it might have been the sound of the river."

"I don't think it was!" Doc told him grimly.

He ran to the gyro, swung into the cockpit and started the motor. He clutched in the rotary wing vanes as rapidly as possible, then bore heavily on the throttle. The strange ship lifted.

Although he had been within the cliff dwelling but a few minutes, the canyon depths were now a good deal less gloomy than before. The explanation was simple. Dawn impended.

Doc guided the ship over the river, and hovered there while he tossed out a flare. The light sank quickly into the stream—but not before he made an interesting discovery.

Near the water's edge, a slab of rock had been toppled back. It had uncovered the entrance of a tunnel, obviously man-made.

Doc wasted no time investigating, except to note a large stake set near the water. To this, a boat had evidently been moored.

What had happened was clear. The builders of the ancient cliff dwelling had constructed the tunnel to give access to water when their stronghold was besieged. Down this, Doc's enemies had fled, to depart in the boat.

How they had closed the tunnel with molten rock was still a mystery—a puzzle Doc hoped to solve by analysis of the air he had trapped in the flask.

He flung the gyro downstream. Caution was necessary to

avoid crashing into the canyon walls. It was doubtful if he made a great deal more speed than had the boat.

The darkness dispersed quickly—dawn comes with suddenness in the clear, dry atmosphere of the West—and he was able to increase his pace.

The river, rushing and angry, abruptly grew more peaceful. The canyon became less sheer, wider. Then there was suddenly no canyon at all, but a gently sloping valley. He was out of the range of mountains through which Red Skull slashed.

A bridge appeared. A graveled highway crossed it. Under the bridge, a large, powerful launch was tied. The cowl and cushions of the boat were still wet with spray.

Two men stood on the bridge. They stared at the strange aircraft approaching them.

Doc landed on the road. He studied the two men as they approached.

One was stout, bulging of shoulder, big of hand. He would have been the better for a shave. His laced boots, khaki breeches, and leather windbreaker had seen much wear. He looked angry.

The second man's attire was that of the city, although his features were leathery from exposure to wind and sun. He had a reddish beard.

"If it isn't one thing, it's another!" the latter greeted Doc. "First, we're robbed of our car. And then you come along in that contraption! What kind of a flyin' machine is that, anyhow?"

Doc passed the question. "Did you get a look at the men who took your car?"

"Just at the one who held the gun—he was Buttons Zortell, a fellow we fired off the job some time ago. He made us lie in the ditch at the side of the road and we didn't see the others. It sounded like there was quite a crowd, though, and I heard a woman's voice. She seemed to be putting up a fight."

This was welcome news, for it meant Lea Aster was still alive.

"Who are you gentlemen?" Doc asked.

"I am Ossip Keller," said the man in city garments. "My companion is my partner, Richard O'Melia."

"You men, together with Nate Raff, own the Mountain Desert Construction Company, don't you?" Doc demanded.

"That's right!"

Doc gestured at the seat beside him. "Get in! We're going after your car—and the men who took it!"

The pair seemed a bit doubtful of the gyroplane. "Will that thing carry us?"

"Of course! And it's much safer than an ordinary plane, if that's worrying you."

The two wedged into the seats. Doc promptly took off.

"The car went north—toward our dam!" said Richard O'Melia in a gruff, roaring voice in keeping with his rough attire.

Doc drove the gyro forward at its maximum speed. Lifting their shouts over the noisy whine of the rotating wings and the shrill of the muffled motor, O'Melia and Keller explained their presence further.

"Our other partner, Nate Raff, was killed in a plane crash yesterday," said O'Melia. "We got an early start this morning, for we've got to go to the crash scene in New Mexico and see if we can identify Nate's body. Every one in the plane was badly burned."

"And Buttons Zortell held us up on the bridge!" O'Melia thundered. "I'm bettin' that's got somethin' to do with Nate's death!"

"What do you mean?" Doc probed.

The men seemed reluctant to commit themselves.

"We suspect foul play in Nate's death!" O'Melia boomed finally.

Ossip Keller now bent a keen-eyed stare on Doc. It was plain to be seen that he was a far more intelligent man than the blustering O'Melia.

"May I ask who you are?" he addressed Doc.

"My name is Savage."

The effect of this was ludicrous. The jaws of both men sagged. They became round-eyed.

"Not Doc Savage?" O'Melia thundered.

"That's right."

"Glory be!" yelled O'Melia. "You're the gent we're wantin' to see more'n anybody! When Nate Raff was killed, he was goin' to New York to see you. We sent Bandy, too!"

"Who was Bandy Stevens?" Doc inquired.

"Didn't Bandy manage to get to you?"

"He did, only to be killed before he could tell me anything."

Ossip Keller now showed a trace of doubt, of suspicion. "If Bandy did not talk to you—why are you here?"

"I'm here because a gang—apparently your enemies—are holding a young woman, the secretary of one of my men!" Doc explained grimly. "You haven't told me who Bandy Stevens was!"

"One of our employees—a man we trusted," Keller answered. "We sent Bandy to enlist your aid. Bandy wired us that some one had shot at him in Phoenix. That worried Nate Raff. So Nate lit out to see you himself—and the plane he was ridin' in crashed."

Doc had been keeping his eyes on the road below. There was plenty of light now, although hills in the east still hid the sun. But no sign of the car could he discern.

"Suppose you gentlemen explain why you were trying to get in touch with me," Doc suggested.

"We've been havin' trouble with our dam buildin'!" thumped O'Melia. "And what trouble! You never saw the like! Rock slides, fatal accidents, equipment failures! Just about everything that could go wrong, did. The thing about it that burns me up is that we didn't suspect no dirty work. But we had to fire too many men for makin' costly mistakes. Buttons Zortell was one of those men. And all of a sudden, we woke up to the fact that somebody was tryin' to break us!"

"For what reason?"

"Blast me if I know! That's the thing that has us up in the air! We got enemies! Every business man has! But our enemies are the kind who would walk up an' take a shot at us, instead of sneakin' around like coyotes."

"Is there any danger of the dam ruining you financially?"

"Danger!" O'Melia wailed. "It's almost done it! We're buildin' this dam out of our own pocket, and it has already cost us twice as much as we figured on. Our treasury is about empty."

"In case of financial failure, what would happen?"

"We'd have to sell out to the highest bidder—sell the partially built dam an' the ground we've bought for the lake, that is. By doin' that, we could salvage our equipment an' start over again."

"Have you received any offers for the uncompleted dam and the lake area?"

O'Melia swore. "One! It wasn't half what it cost us—an' we got it dirt-cheap."

"I thought the dam had cost you plenty?"

"It has! This Nick Clipton just wanted the land. He said he was a rancher."

"Nick Clipton!"

"Sure. He's the jasper who made us the offer."

"Nick Clipton is a fake name used by the master mind who is behind all your trouble!" Doc rapped sharply. "Did you get a look at him when he propositioned you?"

"Naw. The offer came through the mail."

Doc now gave his attention to the terrain below. There was a crossroads immediately ahead. On only one of the four intersection roads was there dust to indicate the recent passage of a vehicle. Doc followed the dust.

"There were some papers or documents involved in the trouble in New York," he announced. "Can you tell me their nature?"

"Probably the dope Bandy carried," O'Melia offered. "He had a letter signed by all three of us, askin' your aid. We also give him maps of the country, plans of the dam, itemized accounts of materials, descriptions of each case of trouble, and so forth. We figured that stuff would be nice for you to study before you got here."

Ossip Keller, taking little part in the conversation, had been staring at Doc steadily. There was an intensity almost irrational in his scrutiny.

"You see, Mister Savage, we took it for granted you would aid us," he now offered. "We had heard great things of you, and the strange life you lead. Or at least it seems a somewhat strange existence to me—your business of traveling to the far corners of the earth to help those who need help."

"And punishing those who have it coming to them!" Doc was moved to add, thinking of Monk's attractive secretary in the hands of Buttons Zortell.

Suddenly, he made a sound of disgust, and whipped the plane around, heading back the way they had come. It was rarely Doc gave any sign of emotion. But this once he was blasted out of his usual calm.

The vehicle making the dust was not the car they sought, but only an empty truck.

THE futility of the dust trail might have been an omen, for, although Doc searched fully two hours, he found no trace of Lea Aster or her captors. He came to the conclusion they had driven into the wooded mountain region and there abandoned their machine in some pine thicket.

He gave up the search. Fuel was running low in the gyro, anyway.

Back over Red Skull Canyon he flew. The great gash looked even more forbidding in the full light of day. O'Melia and Keller were men of strength, yet they clung to the cockpit seats in stiff-armed anxiety lest their conveyance smash into the sheer walls of stone.

The shelf of the landing field, the frowning precipice which held the cliff dwelling, hove into sight.

Men were clustered about Doc's speed plane and the two smaller ships. Doc made a mental count, expecting to enumerate only his five aides. Then he blinked.

The shelf held six men!

The newcomer was perhaps forty years of age, Doc saw as the gyro dropped in for a landing. The man's hair stuck up like cactus thorns. He had an enormous jaw, a lipless mouth, glittering eyes—the effect of the whole being hard-boiled determination. He was powerfully muscled.

A choking sound from his passengers drew Doc's attention. O'Melia and Keller were goggle-eyed with incredulity.

"He didn't die in the plane crash, after all!" O'Melia rasped.

"Who?"

The roughly-clad construction man leveled an arm at the big-jawed stranger among Doc's men.

"That's Nate Raff!" he boomed.

Chapter XIV

THE PLOT SINISTER

SOME two hours after this incident, nine grim and terse-worded men were arrayed in the large corrugated iron shack which was the dam headquarters office. The nine were Doc Savage, his five men, and the three owners of the Mountain Desert concern.

Nate Raff was preparing to tell in detail how he came to be alive in spite of indications that he had perished in the plane wreck. He had already imparted snatches, but not the complete story.

Doc had been too busy to question Raff at length—the two hours since their meeting had been occupied with organizing a search for Lea Aster and her captors. The necessity for this search accounted for Doc's presence so soon at the dam.

Fully half the working force at the dam were now scouring the mountains for the blonde young woman.

Raff wedged a stubby pipe in his lipless mouth. As he talked, he kept the pipe between his teeth. This gave his words a snarling quality. He spoke rapidly, with a sort of fierce energy.

"O'Melia and Keller have told you about our troubles here at the dam, haven't they?" he began. "And how we finally decided, because of the frequency with which things went wrong, that somebody was behind our difficulties. We determined to ask you to come down here and look into the mess. We sent Bandy Stevens to New York for that purpose."

"That much is clear," Doc agreed.

"Well, Bandy wired us he had been shot at in Phoenix, and that worried me," Raff went on. "I started to New York, just to make sure somebody got to you. I took a passenger plane from Phoenix. I like to fly.

"There were other travelers in the plane. After we had been in the air about an hour, one of the passengers drew a gun. He was a squatty gent with a flat nose and cauliflower ears. His name was Jud."

"I met him," Doc said dryly. "Jud is the one who was clever enough to block my efforts to learn the identity of his boss, during my first visit to the cliff dwelling."

"Jud is pretty smart," Raff admitted. "Anyhow, to get back to the plane—Jud made it land. He forced me to go with him, and brought me to that cliff ruin where your men found me."

"And we darn near didn't find you!" Monk put in. "You were in an out-of-the-way room. Anyway, you were tied and gagged, and Doc's anæsthetic gas had overcome you."

"The gang fled so quickly they didn't have time to take me along!" Raff flung through his teeth.

"You did not, at any time, catch sight of the chief of the gang, or hear anything pointing to his real identity?" questioned the dapperly clad Ham, who was sitting to one side, chin and hands resting on his sword cane—his habitual posture when thinking.

"No!" snapped Raff. "I've no idea who he is!"

DOC SAVAGE brought the conversation back to the plane. "You have not accounted for the plane crash, Mister Raff."

Raff chewed his pipe violently. "I can't account for it, either! I don't know what happened!"

"You did not see Jud place a bomb aboard?"

"The only thing I saw Jud do was bust up the radio. He smashed the instruments. Then he ordered the plane to take off. And it did."

"It's evident Jud doctored the ship somehow, causing it to crash!" Ham snapped. "He wanted no witnesses alive to give him trouble later."

"What was their purpose in seizing you, Mister Raff?" Doc asked.

"You've got me!" Raff ejaculated, throwing his hands up in a baffled gesture. "They didn't give any reason. They just held me. I can't understand it!"

"Nor I," Doc echoed grimly.

Doc now drew from a pocket an edition of a Phoenix morning newspaper. It bore the current date. Newspapers were brought from the nearest railroad point by car, and were delivered in the construction camp almost as soon as city dwellers received them.

The sheet had a large story about the plane crash, mostly having to do with efforts to identify the bodies.

"You say Jud took you from the air line?" Doc murmured.

"He sure did!" rasped Raff.

"Then how do you account for the fact that the number of burned bodies found compared exactly with the number of passengers the plane carried?" Doc questioned dryly.

Raff jumped up, his bellow of surprise blowing his pipe from between his teeth. He seized the newspaper and read it to make certain Doc's statement agreed with the printed story. After reading, he sank back in his chair and swore violently.

"I can't explain it!" he yelled. "There should be two missin', because me an' Jud left the plane! But the paper says eleven people were aboard, and eleven bodies found. It's beyond me how the——"

Raff suddenly stopped shouting. He picked up his pipe. A wily look danced in his eyes.

"Here's what I'll bet they done!" he growled. "They doctored the passenger list of the plane to show two less than were aboard!"

"But why, Nate?" asked one of his partners.

"To make it look like I was dead, of course!" Raff retorted. "Then they could keep me prisoner and nobody would know the difference. If they decided to kill me, that would never be suspected, either!"

Doc Savage said nothing for the moment. He moved to the office door and stood gazing idly through it.

Before his eyes stretched orderly streets of board shacks and tents. Several larger structures were labeled as groceries, garages, drug stores. There was even a barn of a hotel set in the midst of them all.

This was the mushroom town occupied by workmen on the Red Skull dam project. Some wag had named the settlement Skullduggery, probably because of the presence of the usual crop of boom town card sharpers and hard characters.

A HUNDRED and fifty or so yards distant stood a tar-papered shack. The windows were boarded over, indicating it was untenanted. The door was closed tightly.

Near by, a trash fire burned. A garage worker had dumped oily rags on this, causing a fog of sooty black smoke. This pall enwrapped the shack, making it seem more deserted than ever.

Despite outward appearances, however, the cabin was far from empty. The single large room was crowded with men. They were the evil individuals who had managed to escape from the cliff dwelling. Only one of their number was missing—their leader was nowhere in evidence.

Five of the gang sat around the edge of a trapdoor in the floor, dangling their legs down. Below was a cellar.

On the hard earth floor of this underground room, Lea Aster lay. She seemed to be sleeping soundly—a little too soundly.

"Supposin' the mohairrie should wake up an' let out a squawk!" muttered one of the men uneasily. "Somebody would sure hear her! We're right in the middle of town."

"She won't wake up!" growled Buttons Zortell. "I gave her enough drug to keep her sleepin' all day!"

"I don't like this hidin' out in the middle of town!" complained Jud, rubbing his hammered-down nose. "And that smoke is chokin' me!"

"Dry up!" Buttons advised him. "It's the last place anybody would look for us."

"Yeah, but supposin' somebody seen us holin' up in here?"

"Nobody did. We got here pretty early, an' we was careful. Anyhow, if we did get found out, we wouldn't have no trouble shootin' our way clear. Not with a third of the men in town on the boss's pay roll, we wouldn't!"

"I didn't know he was organized on that scale!" grunted Jud. "A third of the men! Man, that's costin' him jack! This thing he's after must be worth plenty!"

Buttons Zortell now eyed his fellow thug with sharp curiosity. "Have you been able to figure out what the boss is anglin' for?"

"No!" Jud growled. "I got a cussin' the last time I asked 'im. He's sure keepin' the secret to 'imself!"

Buttons grinned cunningly. "Well, blazes! I ain't lettin' my curiosity get me down! We're gettin' ourn, whether the boss gets his or not! It's gonna be pretty soft for us, too— what with the boss intendin' to take a try himself at gettin' rid of Doc Savage."

"I hope he has better luck than we did!"

"He will! This scheme he's got is a darb! The bronze hombre will be rubbed out—and it'll look like an accident! Even his own men won't suspect! Or if they do smell a rat, they can't prove anything!"

"I'm willin' to lay a bet on the boss!" Jud chuckled. "Come over here an' look!"

Jud had been peering through a tiny slit he had punched in the tar paper which covered a knot hole. From this, he could see through the open door of the distant construction concern office.

IN addition to Doc and his five aides three men were present in the office—the partners who owned the tottering Mountain Desert Construction Company. They had been discussing the troubles of the concern.

O'Melia now arose, gave the belt of his worn khaki breeches a hitch, and scowled. "I gotta get on the job! I'm the foreman of construction here, you know!"

Keller had been staring at the open door, as though in a trance. This glaring at nothing in particular seemed to be a habit with him. He aroused himself, fingered his beard, then stood up.

"I believe I shall also do some work. I have some cost summaries to check over."

"I'll go along and see how much we're in the red!" said Nate Raff, with a macabre attempt at a joke.

The three partners took their departure together. Doc and his five associates were left alone together in the office.

Ham, who had been thinking with his chin on his sword cane, gave vent to a soft whistle.

"I have just been considering what a remarkable coincidence occurred when O'Melia and Keller arrived at that bridge at just the right moment to permit our fleeing enemies to steal their car," he said pointedly.

"Yeah!" Monk scratched the bristles that furred his bullet of a head. "That didn't occur to me!"

"Naturally not!" Ham agreed bitingly.

Monk bent one little, bilious eye on his perpetual pain-in-the-neck. "One of these days, Harvard is gonna lose her lawyer!" he leered.

Ham sniffed, then continued: "Are you sure O'Melia and Keller had a car in the first place, Doc?"

"I have only their word," Doc replied.

"How do they compare in size to the master mind—the fellow in the gabardine coat? Could one or both of them have been at the cliff ruin?"

"Any one of the three partners could have worn the coat," Doc declared. "But that is not proof, or even grounds for suspicion. Furthermore, you must not lose sight of the possibility that the man in the gabardine was not the chief, after all."

"Well, O'Melia and Keller might have been with the gang, and dropped off at the bridge to give us a bum steer," Ham said thoughtfully. "It would verify their story to some degree if we could find the car they say was stolen."

THE car was located within the quarter hour. A phone call came in from a searching party covering one of the mountain roads. The machine had been found in a deep gulch, carefully blanketed with new-cut brush. The smell of gasoline from the abandoned vehicle had led to its discovery. No trace of the men had been found.

"Ham," Doc directed. "You take a finger-print outfit and fly up to the spot in the gyro. See what you can find on the car, in the line of prints."

Twiddling his sword cane, Ham departed on the mission.

At Doc's request, a company shack was assigned to his use. In this, he set up a portable laboratory which was unloaded from the giant speed plane.

An important item in this laboratory was a device for analyzing complex chemical combinations, liquid and vapor, with only a few minutes' work. This mechanism was simple, utilizing the electrical decomposition of the substance under analysis, but the results it secured were equivalent to hours of painstaking work by hand.

With this device, Doc delved into the nature of the flaskful of air he had trapped within the cliff dwelling. He desired to learn the significance of the weird odor. And he hoped this knowledge would tell him what manner of fantastic thing had caused the cliff ruin passage to fill with molten stone!

His first analysis was far from satisfactory. This was demonstrated by the fact that he immediately made another.

He did not apprise his five men, or any one else, of the final outcome of his work.

Doc next went over a record of the difficulties which had beset the building of the dam. Without exception, they were listed either as accidents, or due to somebody's carelessness. Some of the men making costly errors had been discharged. Many were still employed.

Considering the whole roster of troubles, it was evident they had been the working of a systematic plot—not to prevent building of the dam, but to make its construction as costly as possible.

"Somebody is trying to break the concern!" Doc told

the three owners when they assembled for an early afternoon conference. "And I suspect many of your workmen are still on the pay roll of the enemy."

"Blast 'em!" Nate Raff snarled. "We'll fire the whole crew! It's a fine lot of thanks we're gettin'! You know, we started this dam in the first place just to keep our men at work when business got slack!"

"Sale of electrical power would have eventually paid for the project," Doc said shortly.

"After what it's cost us already—it'll never get paid for!" Raff groaned, "Golly, Savage! Can't you get us out of this, somehow?"

"I'll have to be given a free hand," Doc pointed out. "And that will mean myself and my men taking full charge."

"That's what we were hoping you'd do!" Raff said elatedly.

Chapter XV

THE THUNDERING DEATH

ARRANGEMENTS were quickly made, putting Doc Savage and his aides in control of the construction work.

Renny, engineer of impressive repute, took over the mechanical end—the actual work. He was greeted with sour looks by a number of the underforemen, who resented seeing an outsider in authority.

Within an hour, the grumbling stopped. The complaining ones stared in astonishment. Here was a man, they realized, who knew his stuff!

It chanced that an elderly employee on the job had once worked with Renny on a South American bridge job. This man spread hints about Renny's reputation—hints which were not hard to believe, since within his first hour, the big-fisted engineer had made a half dozen changes which would save thousands of dollars in costs.

In the second hour, Renny had a fight. To keep the concrete cool while it was in process of settling—a necessity because of the heat generated in the setting process—water was circulated through numerous pipes set in the dam body. These pipes became a part of the dam, and later would be pumped full of grout, or thin mortar. But at the present moment, they were carrying water which was chilled in a refrigerating plant.

The plant attendant, a gangling giant almost as big as Renny, let the ammonia compressors overheat. As a result, a bearing froze. Renny raised a roar that could have been heard a mile—not an uncommon performance for a construction man.

The attendant took a swing at Renny—and awakened in the camp hospital four hours later. For the next week, the fellow maintained he had been hit by no human fist—it could have been nothing less than a sixteen-pound rock hammer. Eye-witness testimony was to the contrary.

Examining the ammonia compressor oil, Renny found it was not oil at all, but a compound in imitation, which had no lubrication qualities whatever. This accounted for the burned bearings.

Renny promptly stopped work. He gathered all the workmen—even having the night force routed out of bed. Then he read the riot act to them.

His huge fists, parked like rusty kegs on his hips, he told them what was what—that somebody was trying to break the Mountain Desert Company, and spending plenty of money to do it.

"I'm not wasting the breath to tell you it's gonna stop!" he finished. "I'm just blasted well warning you that you'd better not be caught! It won't be healthy! In fact, it'll be blame fatal!"

This was taken by the construction men in sober-faced silence. They seemed to realize the full seriousness of the situation. Not a smile appeared. The quiet was like that in a courtroom waiting for a death sentence to be pronounced.

Then somebody in the rear gave Renny a loud bird.

Renny stormed into the crowd in search of the jokester, but didn't find him.

As a matter of fact, it had been Ham, who had happened along in time to hear Renny's dramatic declaration. He couldn't resist the opportunity.

HAM had just returned from his mission to get the finger prints off the car stolen from Keller and O'Melia.

"Finger prints had been wiped off the wheel, door handles, emergency brake, and so forth," he reported to Doc Savage in the improvised laboratory. "There wasn't a thing of value."

"All right," Doc replied. "I'm going to have a look around."

He stepped out of the laboratory. Several persons, workmen off duty or hangers-on about the mushroom town of Skullduggery, stared at him.

Doc had removed the make-up used during the night, restoring the natural bronze color of his skin. This, coupled with his remarkable proportions and notable bearing, was what drew attention. He was a man who commanded interest.

Of all those who saw Doc striding along the construction camp street, probably no one was more impressed than Buttons Zortell. The scar-cheeked villain drew his eye from the peephole in the wall of his shack hiding place.

"Blazes!" he muttered. "The bronze guy is finally goin' down to the job! That'll give the boss his chance!"

Jud chuckled dryly. "Fifty bucks says this is the last time we ever see Doc Savage!" he offered.

Buttons snorted. "You want a sure thing!"

This drew a round of mirth from the other men, some of whom were sprawled on the floor. Others sat in the cellar where it was less smoky, and where they could keep an eye on Lea Aster.

A truck rumbled along the street, laden with sacked cement.

Doc hitched a ride on the vehicle. The truck followed a curving, rutty, rather steep road which wound down to the dam scene.

Doc alighted near the workings, leaving the truck to continue on to the great battery of concrete mixers. Danger seemed farthest from his mind as he stood on the site of a spillway and took in the spectacle.

Coffer dams, erected above and below the main construction, held back the water. Big pumps kept the space between the coffers fairly dry. The river was diverted through tunnels in either wall of the chasm. These would later serve to carry water to the power houses.

On cables, slung across the canyon, traveled basketlike cars, sometimes called "storks." The nickname probably came from the dizzy rides they offered. They had been erected to ferry the workmen from the opposite side at the hour when shift changed.

Near by, power shovels were mucking rock into trucks; a bit farther on scalers were working on the cliff with jackhammers and drills, setting powder shots. This work had to do with opening a road which was to cross the dam.

Doc moved in search of Monk.

A CATERPILLAR tractor with a "bulldozer" on the front and a "cowdozer" on the rear was pushing loose rock into piles for the mucking shovels.

Over the whole scene rolled the rattle and clank and scream of machinery, the whine of motors, the chugging of trucks, the clattery gurgle of concrete, the shouts of bosses. Dust squirmed in clouds.

The heat was terrific. Practically none of the workmen wore shirts, and the sun had burned them brown as Indians.

Monk was slung down the dam face. With the aid of two scalers—men who had formerly been circus acrobats—he was sinking small holes into the concrete and taking samples. Later the holes would be filled with grout under pressure.

"Everything seems to be O. K. so far," he reported.

Monk's assigned job was to ascertain whether any faulty material had gone into construction—material which might later cause the great barrier to give way. His ability as a chemist fitted him for this work.

High up on the abysmal walls, Doc could discern Johnny. The lanky geologist was moving about like a granddaddy-long-legs. He carried his spectacles with the magnifying left lens in one hand, a prospector's hammer in the other. A bag for rock specimens was slung over his shoulder and bounced around as he climbed the cliff.

Johnny was seeking the cause of mysterious rock slides which had not only destroyed valuable machinery at various times, but had crushed four workmen to death. Apparently solid areas of stone had a habit of giving away for no explainable reason, according to reports.

What caused this, Johnny was pretty certain to learn. Few men knew more about the structure of the earth than did Johnny.

Doc took an elevator down to the rear of the dam, and made for the power houses. These were two in number, one on each side of the river, and were only partially built. Installation of the turbines and generators had yet to be attended to.

Long Tom, the electrical wizard, had taken charge of this phase of the work. Doc found him in the left-hand power house, grumbling because his favorite type of equipment was not being installed.

"And there's another thing!" he informed Doc. "The bases they've installed cannot be used for the type of turbines they've ordered. Changes will have to be made, at a cost of fifteen or twenty thousand dollars."

"We'll check up on the mistake!" Doc said grimly. "I want to question whoever is responsible. We'll learn some-how who is behind all this sabotage."

"I'll make inquiries," Long Tom declared.

Leaving the power house, Doc strode along below the beetling cliff. Sunbaked muck of the dry river bed was underfoot. The stream had been hardly more than fifty feet wide here. The dark rock sides rose almost vertically.

Overhead, the wire hawsers of the cable cars draped like scattered, huge cobwebs.

A sharp thump of an explosion sounded. Doc glanced around—up. An appalling sight met his gaze.

The entire frowning chasm wall seemed to be sliding down upon him!

IT was a rock slide of tremendous proportions. It extended for many yards in either direction. And enough stone was coming down to fill the entire stream bed.

Escape seemed a fantastic thought. Outrunning the avalanche was an impossibility. Scaling the opposite wall of the canyon was also beyond hope—it was rock worn glass-smooth by the rushing waters of ages.

Doc lost no time in aimless staring or speculation. He went into action as though he had practiced this very thing a thousand times. His hand flicked out the silk cord and grapple. He flung it upward.

A single cable line of the many above was not anchored in the sliding wall. This hawser extended from a point near the dam, diagonally down to the power house, which was just beyond the slide area.

The grapple seemed hardly to touch the aërial hawser before Doc was dangling from the silken cord, hauling himself up. Even then, he was none too quick. A boulder, leaping in advance of the rest, struck him. His bronze form swung like a penny on a string.

Roaring, cracking, grinding with cataclysmic fury, the slide piled into the canyon bed. Rocks the size of houses bounced like marbles and smashed like snowballs. Dust vomited from the débris. It enveloped Doc's rapidly climbing form.

The canyon quaked to the reverberations of rending stone. The dust spread and spread until it swathed even the dam scene itself in a choking fog. The slide was doing no damage to the dam, though.

Workmen, unable to tell the extent of the slide, became panic-stricken and fled their jobs. Yelling, cursing, they fought each other to be first up the truck roads.

Suddenly, out of the dust haze enveloping the dam terminus of the power house cableway, a mighty bronze man appeared. His voice, crashing through the confusion with an uncanny power, arrested frightened men in their tracks. They listened to the bronze giant's orders, and sheepish looks came to their faces. They returned.

Ambulances and fire wagons came caterwauling down the crooked road from Skullduggery. Women, whose menfolk were employed on the dam, trailed these in a hysterical horde.

An ambulance driver failed to allow enough for a turn. As a result, his vehicle rolled over twice, without leaving the road. They hauled the driver out with a broken arm.

Amazingly enough, this man suffered the most drastic injury produced by the gigantic rock slide. There were numerous bruises, minor cuts, and a few black eyes and skinned knuckles—the latter among fellows who had fought to be first to imagined safety. But not a man had perished in the slide.

Doc, upon learning the latter fact, took a curious viewpoint.

"It looks to me as if a lot of the workmen might have been expecting this—and kept out of danger!" he informed Monk.

At this point, a burst of excited shouts drew Doc's attention. He ran for the sound, rounded a spur of rock—and surprised halted him.

Johnny had his gaunt frame sprawled atop a prone man. The pair had evidently been fighting, with Johnny the victor.

"What's the trouble, Johnny?" Doc demanded.

"I caught this bird runnin' from the place where the rock slide started!" gritted the bony geologist. "I think he caused it!"

Doc shifted to get a view of the prisoner's features.

It was the red-whiskered member of the partner trio— Ossip Keller!

Chapter XVI

NEW SUSPECT

"THAT'S a blasted lie!" Ossip Keller bellowed. "I didn't have a thing to do with the slide!"

Johnny arose, but retained a tight grip on Keller's coat. "You were running away, though!"

"Sure I ran!" Keller said angrily. "Who wouldn't! I thought it was an earthquake, or somethin'!"

Twisting, he threw a fist at Johnny's rail-thin midriff. The fist missed. The next instant there was a clank as of two wooden blocks colliding. Keller fell down. He sat there, feeling of his jaw and eying Johnny's knuckles as though he had never seen such things.

"Getting tough won't help you!" Doc advised Keller. "Better behave yourself. I'll be back in a minute."

He ran over to the point where the slide had started and began an investigation.

Without trouble, he found where an explosive—probably a quart or so of nitroglycerin—had been detonated. This had probably been the sharp blast which immediately preceded the slide.

Doc's golden eyes held dissatisfied gleamings. This comparatively small shot had not released those thousands of tons of stone! He glanced about. The rock looked entirely solid. It was dark stuff, with here and there a veining of lighter hue.

These veins received the bronze man's attention. He risked death by clambering a few yards down the abrupt face from which the slide had broken.

He made an intensive examination, employing a small pocket microscope and various chemicals.

Once his eerie trilling note came into momentary being, rising and falling in not unmusical crescendo, but so vague and indefinable that a listener would have been driven to the belief that it was an imaginative figment. Only Doc's five trusted aides would have known from whence the mellow note filtered. Only they would have understood that it meant Doc had made an interesting discovery.

Doc returned to where Johnny was holding the irate Ossip Keller.

"I can't understand how a slide like that occurred in this rock formation!" Johnny complained, with the concern of a geologist who sees all laws of his world violated. "I would swear it couldn't happen!"

"The explosion of a small quantity of nitro started the slide," Doc offered.

Johnny adjusted his spectacles with the magnifying left lens. He blinked owlishly at Doc. "That slide was a geological impossibility, and you know it! I don't see how it could possibly have happened!"

"Granted, Johnny. Have you noticed the veining in the stone, though?"

"Of course."

"And you realize there are chemical combinations which would dissolve the filling of those veins, or at least weaken it greatly."

Johnny stared. "Is that——"

"It is. Some one has induced chemical solutions into the veining, causing the entire rock formation to weaken. The blast of nitro merely set it into motion."

Johnny scowled darkly at Ossip Keller. "This man was acting suspiciously in the vicinity of the slide! He can't deny that!"

OSSIP KELLER was purple with rage. His red beard stuck out like cat whiskers. Evidently being manhandled on his own property was something new in his experience.

He began to express a profane opinion of Doc and the world in general, but caught the big bronze man's eye and hastily changed his attitude.

"I had nothing to do with the slide!" he insisted once more. "If somebody set off a blast, I didn't see it. But I did hear the noise of all that rock going down."

He paused to shiver violently. "It scared me. I may as well admit it. It scared me stiff—and that was why I was running."

"Why'd you fight me when I tried to stop you?" Johnny demanded skeptically.

Keller was perspiring. "I was frightened—the sound of that slide resembled an earthquake. I was in a quake once, and was badly injured. I have a horror of them. When I heard that rumbling and roaring and saw all the dust, it terrified me." A pronounced shudder racked him.

"You can go," Doc said dryly. "We'll accept your story for the time being."

Ossip Keller glared at Johnny. "You gotta apologize to me, mister!"

Johnny snorted. "Listen, Keller—when an apology is due, you'll get it. If you start bellowing for one before that time —you'll get this!" And the lanky geologist shoved out a cluster of hard knuckles.

Keller wet his lips a time or two, then departed, stamping a little to maintain his shaken dignity.

"There's one bird who is wishing he hadn't called on us for help!" Johnny grinned. "What do you make of his story, Doc? Sounded thin to me."

"Have you noticed his habit of staring blankly at objects?" Doc countered.

"What's that got to do with his story?"

"His trancelike behavior indicates he is given to moods, and is possibly the victim of a minor mental disorder."

"You mean he's half nuts?"

"Oh, no. He's just the kind who would fly all to pieces under sudden excitement—such as that slide. His earthquake mania story, if true, would account for his behavior."

"And if it wasn't true—it would account for a lot more!"

"You can add him to your suspect list, if it'll make you feel any better," Doc said amiably.

Johnny squinted over his glasses. "Speaking of suspect lists, who is on yours, Doc?"

"You'd be surprised!" Doc replied.

No levity underlay Doc's seemingly flippant reply; indeed,

his tone was as dry and cold as it ever became. Johnny, noting this fact, felt a surge of elation. He was suddenly certain that Doc had formed definite ideas as to the master mind's identity. The big bronze man must be even now seeking the necessary proof.

And there was still Lea Aster. Her rescue came before everything else.

Johnny took off his glasses, cleaned them. His hands showed nervousness by moving jerkily. Thought of Lea Aster had upset him. It was strange their enemies had not tried to use the young woman's safety as a club to drive Doc off the scene. Did this mean she was no longer alive?

JOHNNY's fears were groundless. Word reached them from Lea Aster shortly before dusk. The manner of its reaching them was suspicious.

Doc Savage had a faculty for seeing all that went on about him, without seeming to do so. Hence it was that he observed roughly clad Richard O'Melia in the act of furtively dropping something behind a desk.

O'Melia seemed nervous. Immediately after he concealed the object, he glanced around. Doc was apparently reading a newspaper. O'Melia did not notice a small mirror in the palm of Doc's hand. But the mirror relayed every move of the man as he hurriedly quit the office.

Doc glided over and secured the article O'Melia had secreted. It was an envelope. It bore Doc's name—written in the firm hand of Lea Aster. It was unsealed.

A bronze flash, Doc reached the door. "O'Melia!"

The burly construction man wheeled nervously.

Doc indicated the envelope. "Didn't you lose this?"

O'Melia's mouth opened and shut. His fingers fidgeted until he jammed them deep in the pockets of his laced khaki breeches. He seemed in pain.

"So you saw me ditch it!" he muttered. "I was afraid of that! Now I'm in a sure-enough jam!"

"Why?"

"Read it and you'll see."

"First," Doc clipped grimly, "where did you get it?"

"I found it in my pocket!" O'Melia said earnestly. "That's the truth, believe it or not! I don't know how it got there. But I think somebody wanted to get the message to you, and tried to throw suspicion on me in the bargain."

"Why did you try to hide it?"

O'Melia squirmed like a boy caught pilfering a melon patch. Either he was a good actor and liar—or genuinely uneasy.

"It gave me the jitters, findin' it in my pocket that way!" he explained. "I was gonna figure out some way of gettin' it in your hands without showin' it come from me—I mean —that I ever had it!"

Doc drew out the contents of the envelope—a single sheet of cheap tablet paper.

On it, Lea Aster had penned a message:

MR. SAVAGE: I am being forced to write this, naturally.

I am asked to convey to you the information that, should you be in Arizona to-morrow morning, you will get a package containing my left hand. My other hand will reach you at noon. Each six hours thereafter, if you remain in the State, some part of me will be chopped off and sent you as a reminder.

I am in deadly danger here. Please do what they wish.

LEA ASTER.

Doc's five men, accompanied by Ossip Keller and Nate Raff, came in. Doc handed them the missive, saying nothing. Then he stepped out of the office, hurried to the temporary laboratory, and got the lantern which created ultra-violet light.

There was a chance Lea Aster had chalked a secret message upon the paper.

OSSIP KELLER scowled at Doc as he came in with the box-like lantern. It was plain, Keller still boiled with rage because of his encounter with Johnny. His indignation was the natural state of mind for a righteous man. But it was impossible to tell whether he was really affronted, or wearing his cloak of wrath to cover more sinister feelings.

The flimsy buildings of Skullduggery were wired with regular lighting current, supplied by the company plant at the dam site. Doc plugged in the ultra-violet lantern. Had there been no other current available, a few moments' work would have changed the lantern to battery operation.

Lea Aster's note received the invisible beams.

"Glory be!" Monk chortled.

Eerie blue lettering had appeared upon the paper. Glowing with a curious, electric quality, it was easily readable:

This message is a bluff, Doc. They intend to keep me unharmed and use me to force you to release any of the gang you should happen to capture.

I have not been able to learn who is the brains back of this. His name is never mentioned in my hearing.

I have no idea where I am being held.

Monk emitted a long, gusty sigh of relief. "I'm sure glad the note was only a bluff! It had me worried for a minute."

"They're clever to use the girl as they are!" Doc said gravely. "This way, they hinder my operations considerably."

Surprise leaped upon Monk's homely face. "But this is the first time they have threatened to do bodily harm to her——"

"They didn't need to threaten," Doc indicated. "And they know that, no doubt. There are numerous workmen on the dam who are obviously in the gang. The fellow who let the ammonia compressor in the refrigerating plant overheat is an example—he was not so dumb but that he knew he wasn't using oil in the bearings. And there are others like him. Yet it is necessary for me to refrain from seizing them.

"The moment I capture one of the gang, things will come to a show-down. Either I'll have to turn my prisoner loose, or the girl will be killed. But as long as I have not actually trapped some of them, they're not likely to harm Miss Aster. She is, in fact, their trump card—for use only in a crisis! They surely know that."

Doc's five men showed marked relief as they heard these theories expounded.

Others did not look so free of mind. O'Melia and Keller —toward whom suspicion already pointed—shifted uneasily in their tracks. They seemed not to know what to do with their hands. Both perspired freely, but that might have been due to the heat.

Nate Raff stood apart, big jaw outthrust, pipe clamped in his lipless mouth. His gaze fell on his two partners and lingered curiously. Even he could see all was not well with the pair. Suddenly he looked away, as though to conceal a swift, horrible suspicion.

Doc's five aides were men trained in the quiet observation of details. They saw Nate Raff's expression. They read its meaning as clearly as though Raff had been an actor registering feeling before a camera.

Raff's look had shown that he suspected one or the other of his partners!

Chapter XVII
CLEW TRAIL

So tense was the situation that no one noticed Doc Savage was again examining the note from Lea Aster. His attention was centered on the paper itself, and the envelope. A pocket microscope was in use.

On the underside of the paper, he found faint, dark smears. These had come from the table upon which the paper had been placed while being written upon. The nature of no material could defy Doc's analysis for long. He soon knew what the stains were.

Soot from oil smoke!

Without a word, he quitted the office. He wasted no time. His remarkable faculty for deduction had already functioned. He knew what the soot meant.

Skullduggery, being a temporary city, had no buildings equipped with oil furnaces. Mesquite stems served as firewood. These did not make an oily smoke. Doc had noted a trash fire not far distant, and the dark smoke it exuded. The fire no longer burned, but he recalled its location.

More important, he remembered that only one shack had been in the path of smoke from the conflagration. In this, it was reasonable to believe, the girl had written the note.

A thicket of mesquite received Doc's figure. He seemed to vanish in the gnarled growth. A darkening twilight helped his disappearance.

All was quiet about the tar-paper shack which had served Lea Aster's captors as a refuge. No light showed through the boarded windows.

Three or four striped gophers played around the doorstep. Atop the roof, a woodpecker operated industriously on a wormhole. Peace reigned.

A moist, jingly plop sounded near the shack. After this, the playful gophers seemed to go to sleep. The woodpecker lay down.

Inside the building, two loud thumps might have been the noise of men falling out of chairs.

Doc Savage, big and bronze, appeared as if by magic before a mesquite clump. He ran for the hut.

His remarkable anæsthetic gas had already done its work and become harmless. Its penetration into the flimsy shack had been swift, thanks to cracks in the rickety walls. It had spread instant unconsciousness—a coma which would eventually pass, leaving the victims entirely unharmed.

Doc reached the door, but did not grasp the knob. His flashlight dispelled the gloom for a moment. The knob had a sticky, sirupy coating.

Once more had Doc's habitual caution saved him. The stuff on the knob was undoubtedly poison such as had slain Bandy Stevens!

AROUND to the end of the shack glided the bronze giant. His right hand became a hard, metallic block. It smashed once. A plank caved with a splintering crash. Grasping other planks, Doc tore them off.

It was an amazing feat. With his bare hands, he did a job which seemingly called for axes and wrecking bars. The hardwood planks might have been strawberry boxes, from the way they yielded to his case-hardened bronze fingers.

He entered, his flashlight gushing whiteness.

Two men were heaped on the floor. Both lay face down. Both snored noisily.

Doc brushed them with a toe, turning them. They were two of the cliff-dwelling gang.

The flash beam, hunting like a hungry thing, located a trapdoor in the floor. Doc opened this. Steps led down into an earth-walled cellar.

The cellar floor was littered with cigarette stubs, pipe dottle, burned matches.

No one was there. Doc descended and searched but found nothing of value. The cigarettes were all hand-rolled, cowboy fashion. The matches were grocery-store variety.

A rough table upstairs held a five-cent tablet. From this, the paper for Lea Aster's note had obviously come. All signs indicated the cabin had harbored a crowd of men through the day.

The gang had retired to some other- retreat, taking their young woman prisoner. Only two of their number had been left behind.

Doc Savage scooped up the two prisoners. They seemed without weight in his powerful grasp. He pushed them out through the hole he had torn, then followed himself. He cleaned the poison off the front door knob with a handkerchief taken from one of his captives. He burned the handkerchief.

The increasing darkness then swallowed him. He carried the unconscious men.

Thunder gave a sudden thump in the distance, then rolled across the heavens like the insane laughter of a man half choked. Lightning batted a red eye. A wind, stifling hot, scurried across the canyons and mesas. Overhead, clouds were massed in blowsy, awesome battalions.

A turbulent, threatful night promised.

THE three partners who owned the Mountain Desert Construction Company were still in the office. Doc's men were with them.

They stared their surprise when Doc strode in with his two captives.

"Where'd you get 'em?" Monk demanded.

Doc explained. He placed the two senseless men on separate desks.

"We'll make them talk," he finished. "Watch them while I go get the serum from the laboratory."

He left the room quickly.

"Serum—serum!" Nate Raff gave his enormous jaw a puzzled tug. "What did Savage mean by that?"

"Truth serum," Monk replied, as if surprised that Raff did not comprehend.

"But I didn't think that stuff was reliable," Raff objected. "Police are not allowed to use confessions obtained by its use!"

"You watch!" Monk grinned. "Doc uses hypnotism after he administers the stuff. These two birds will spill everything they know!"

Thunder whooped noisily overhead as Monk spoke. It was as if some ethereal colossus had been tickled. Lightning sprayed red flame over desert and mountain.

For a moment, the boisterous elements commanded attention. For ten seconds or so, the two senseless captives were forgotten!

During that interval, a sharp eye might have seen each man give a small twitch. A single sharp movement—as though a horrible agony had penetrated through the stupor of their slumber.

Amid the gobbling uproar of the thunder overhead, none noticed the two unconscious men had stopped breathing!

Not until Doc Savage returned was the truth known. The bronze man halted the instant he caught sight of the two on the desks.

"They're dead!" he said sharply.

Had lightning struck the flimsy building, the shock would not have been greater.

"They can't be!" roared Nate Raff. "We've been here all the time!"

"All the time!" echoed O'Melia, hitching nervously at his khaki breeches. "Yes, sir!"

"Maybe your anæsthetic killed 'em!" red-bearded Keller told Doc in a surly mutter.

Renny started for the dead men.

"Don't!" Doc warned.

With quick gestures, he indicated the peril of going near the bodies. Splattered across the features of each unfortunate were sirupy stains.

"The poison which kills on contact!" he announced.

"But where did it come from?" Nate Raff thundered.

The office windows were open. Outside one of them, Doc found the answer to Raff's query. A toy water pistol! From this, the fatal liquid had been squirted. It was wiped clean of finger prints.

"Somebody let 'em have it through the window!" boomed Raff.

Keller nodded and explored his red whiskers with his trembly fingers. O'Melia shivered.

But grim looks passed among the aides of Doc Savage. They were trained observers, these five men. Although at times they might seem as children compared to the mighty bronze man who was their leader, each of the five had an unusually keen brain. They ranked as high above an ordinary man as they themselves were topped by their amazing bronze chief.

Every one of them saw that no tracks were outside the window where the water pistol lay! They realized the water gun had been thrown from inside the office. They knew one of the Mountain Desert partners had killed the two so they couldn't be questioned.

The discovery appalled them. Raff, O'Melia, Keller—which man was it? The question baffled them.

They wondered if Doc had singled out one man in his mind as the culprit. Why was he holding his hand? Was it to rescue Lea Aster? Was it to learn what was back of the crimes? Was it to solve the mystery of the red-hot lava in the ancient cliff dwelling?

Doc Savage, bronze and inscrutable, voiced no answers.

Soon after the bodies had been removed, Doc requested quarters. He and his men were assigned a long corrugated iron building, one of many similar structures which lined a Skullduggery street.

It was situated a short distance from the shack which Doc had already taken over as a laboratory.

Horror, peril, death—none of these visibly affected Doc Savage. He retired to the new quarters, lay down and slept.

The satanic bedlam in the sky did not bother him. The whizzing cracks and cannonading of lightning, the stifling heat, the tinkle of wind-carried sand against the corrugated iron building, failed to disturb him.

Four hours later, he arose. The minimum of slumber had refreshed him, and tuned up his faculties for the dangerous work ahead.

Before dressing, Doc took his exercises. This was a grueling routine and lasted almost two hours. It was unlike anything else in the world. Doc's father had started him on the ritual when he could hardly walk, and Doc had continued it religiously from that day.

To these exercises could be laid the credit for Doc's tremendous physical and mental powers. He made his muscles tug against each other in a fashion he had perfected, until perspiration covered his mighty bronze body in a heavy film.

He selected a number of a dozen figures and juggled it mentally, multiplying, dividing, extracting square and cube roots. This whetted his powers of concentration.

He carried with him always an apparatus which made sound waves of frequencies so high and low the ordinary human ear could not detect them. Through a lifetime of practice, Doc had perfected his ears to a point where the sounds registered. He named scores of assorted odors after a quick olefactory test of small vials racked in a special case.

To sharpen his touch, he read pages of very fine Braille printing—the writing for the blind which is a system of up-raised dots.

He had many other varied parts in his routine. He went through them at a terrific pace, giving himself no time for rest. Dressing, he stepped out into the night.

Lightning splashed; thunder made the earth tremble. The wind had died and it was hotter. The clouds overhead were blue-black, bloated, threatening.

Doc swung off in the direction of the dam.

Two men watched him go. Scowls distorted their faces. Both held rifles, and the grips of single-action six-shooters stuck hornlike from low-slung holsters.

One gargled a curse and leveled his Winchester in Doc's direction.

The other man caught his arm. "Nix, Jud! You might miss!"

"You're crazy, Buttons!" growled the other. "I can get a bead on 'im durin' one of these lightnin' flashes! I'm a crack shot!"

"Don't take the chance!" Buttons snapped. "We've got an-other way of doin' it!"

The skulking pair allowed five minutes for Doc Savage to get out of the vicinity. Then they crept into a mesquite thicket and came out carrying a barrel. They handled this barrel very gingerly indeed. Toward Doc's quarters, they bore it.

Under the eaves of the long corrugated building stood an-other barrel, used to catch rain water for washing purposes.

The barrel carried by Buttons Zortell and Jud exactly matched the one which belonged under the eaves. They made a quick exchange.

Only a close examination would reveal the substitution.

And who would take the trouble of scrutinizing a harmless rain barrel?

"They can even dip wash water out without noticin' anything wrong!" Buttons chuckled, as they bore the other barrel away.

"Will we let 'er go soon as the bronze guy comes back here?" Jud wanted to know.

Buttons considered this deeply. "It'd be better if we could get his five pals with 'im! We'll try to do that!"

The sky suddenly roared with thunder.

Jud, looking up, chuckled. "There's sure gonna be a cloudburst!"

"That makes it swell for us, huh?" Buttons laughed.

But Jud was not so certain. "The thing ain't gonna be easy to do!"

"Blazes! All we gotta do is sit out here until we see Savage go into the shack, along with his men, then——"

"I don't mean that!" Jud snapped. "I'm talkin' about the business at the dam! Savage is gonna be on the job! Somebody may get caught!"

"Well, it won't be us!" Buttons grunted callously. "We ain't handlin' that end."

Jud seemed to struggle with his supply of brain matter, forcing it to wrestle with a mystery. The lightning flashes showed his inch-wide brow ditched with wrinkles. He gave it up.

"I don't savvy it!" he grumbled.

"Savvy what?"

"Why the boss don't go ahead an' blow up the dam. That would put the company out of business! Why's he doin' this other thing?"

"The boss is after somethin'!" Buttons explained patiently. "Can't you get that through your head? It's somethin' nobody but him knows about! He knows what he's doin'!"

The two ceased their somewhat vague conversation. They settled themselves to wait. Their job was here. They were the human triggers of a death trap.

At the dam, another sinister plot was proceeding. A plot, it seemed, which did not have to do with destruction of the dam!

Chapter XVIII
MYSTERIOUS MOTIVES

Doc Savage created a stir of interest when he appeared on the dam scene. Somebody had dug up the magazine section of a Sunday newspaper, published some weeks previously. This contained a story by a feature writer who had an imagination and a big supply of glowing adjectives. The story had to do with Doc Savage—man of mystery, wizard of science, muscular superman.

Among other things, the feature story speculated about the bronze man's source of fabulous wealth. At irregular intervals, said the tale, mysterious shipments of gold came to Doc. These shipments were stupendous of sum—as much as five million dollars.

The yarn would have sounded a bit fantastic had it carried the truth about Doc's golden trove. At noon on a prescribed day of each week, Doc had but to broadcast, over powerful radio stations, a few words in a mysterious tongue. Some days later, the gold would arrive.

The wealth came from a hidden valley in Central America, a lost retreat presided over by descendents of the ancient Mayan race, and was supplied Doc solely for the purpose of furthering his cause of right. Few people knew this, however.

The newspaper feature had given Doc a reputation among the dam workmen. Many were the curious stares which followed him about.

Salvos of thunder romped across the heavens, the echoes filling the great canyon with a steady clamor. Lightning was coming so often now that the sky seemed an inverted, bloody bowl.

Doc found Renny directing the placing of tarpaulins over the newly poured concrete.

"It don't rain in this country, they tell me," Renny said. "The sky just falls on you!"

Workmen were moving up out of the canyon. Squads staked covers over electrical equipment, and made lumber fast. They had had experience with Western cloudbursts.

The strings of electric bulbs—they were mounted in rough-and-ready reflectors made of common tin dishpans—seemed to become paler and paler as the blaze of lightning increased. It became so that men could perform their allotted tasks independent of the electric lights.

The earth seemed to tremble in terror of the heavenly theatrics. The sky seemed to press down. Clouds boiled like black, tortured foam.

Suddenly the rain came. Not drops, not sheets, but in a roaring mass. The chasm walls turned into vertical torrents. Shovels, chipping hammers, clay diggers, picks—all sorts of loose tools, were dashed down the sheer stone walls. Sacked concrete, boulders as large as tubs, rolled over and over in the flood.

Then came two jarring explosions. Real blasts, these! Manmade!

"Holy cow!" Renny groaned. "They have blown up the diversion tunnels!"

Doc did not answer. The moaning inferno of the cloudburst was no place to carry on a conversation.

The storm moved in an upstream direction—out over the ancient lake bed which was to be flooded by the Red Skull dam. They were strange things, these Western cloudbursts. They emptied prodigious quantities of water. And Doc had never experienced a more violent one than this.

Moving along the dam, he located the cableway which led down to the power houses. The flood had put the power lines out of commission, however, and the car would not operate.

He tried the phone—different parts of the job were connected by telephone. These still functioned. He put a call down to the power houses.

"How much water is coming through the diversion tunnels?" he asked.

"None!" was the report. "Explosions seem to have closed 'em up above the dam!"

Doc hung up. He stood in the little phone shed, listening to water flood against the corrugated iron. A thoughtful expression gripped his features.

An explosion could have destroyed the dam as readily as the diversion tunnels had been closed. The stoppage of the diversion tunnels meant the dam would have to hold water. These tunnels merely carried the stream around the structure. Their closure was a minor calamity—if the dam held. And it should, providing the water didn't get too high, which was highly unlikely.

Why seek to get water in the dam? That was the puzzle Doc considered.

And he apparently found a satisfactory answer, for there came from his lips the low, mellow, trilling sound—the small, unconscious thing which he did when something of marked importance had occurred. Melodious, yet devoid of tune, the weird note mingled defiantly with the deafening bellow of the cloudburst.

The rainfall began to slacken. It became a normal downpour, then a hard rain. This seemed but a dew, compared to that which had gone before. But, out on the lake bed, the cloudburst continued.

From Skullduggery, the three owners of the construction company came running. They were excited. If one of them felt something besides concern over the safety of the dam, he failed to show it.

Water, uneasy and foam-flecked, had already climbed many feet up the cement-and-steel barrier.

"If it just don't give way!" Nate Raff wailed. "If it just don't! The concrete is awful green!"

"It's lucky you used a quick-set concrete!" Renny told him. "That may save it! But you can bet there's going to be a lot of water in there before mornin'!"

Renny was an excellent prophet. The cloudburst hung roaring and flashing over the lake bed, then crept on into the waste of mesas and canyons which drained into the lake. The water level kept climbing, inches to the minute at first, then more slowly.

"The dam is going to hold!" was Doc's final verdict.

The hour was well past midnight. Renny, for all his tremendous muscular development, was dog tired. Monk and Ham were too played out to do more than give each other uncivil looks. Long Tom and Johnny were not so exhausted —Long Tom because he had done no hard work, and Johnny because it was next to impossible to wear him out. Johnny, little more than a framework of tendon-armored bones, had been known to travel for days without sleep, and with only a little water to drink.

In view of the fact that Doc had captured his sleep in the early evening, the other five hardly expected him to turn in with them now. They were surprised when he did.

A silently thoughtful group, they entered the long corrugated shack, which had been assigned them as quarters.

Buttons Zortell and Jud, soaking wet from the cloudburst, observed from their mesquite clump. They put their heads close together, so as to converse in the faintest of whispers.

"Now is your chance!" said Jud.

"*Your* chance, you mean!" growled Buttons.

"Blast it!" Jud snarled. "You ain't gonna shove it off onto me! There's some risk!"

"We'll match for it, then."

"Fair enough."

Buttons now thrust a hand in his pocket, brought it out, and shoved it, a closed fist, into Jud's clutch.

"How many coins in my hand—one or two?" he asked. "If you guess wrong, you gotta go."

Jud smiled slyly in the darkness. He had heard a click in Buttons's hand, and knew there were two coins. "Two!" he said.

It was Buttons's turn to smirk. There was only one coin, and he had clicked it against a ring he was wearing to make it sound like two.

Grumbling, and wondering how he had been so mistaken,

Jud started for the building housing Doc's group. Then he scuttled back.

"Here comes a truck, dang it!"

THE truck, skidding on the rain-hammered roadway, groaned up to Doc's quarters. It had a vanlike body. Engine howling, it turned and backed up to the door.

Numerous boxes were unloaded.

"Must be some stuff Savage had shipped out by rail from New York?" Jud ruminated.

"He ain't gonna need it!" Buttons grated.

The truck soon drove away.

Clouds came unexpectedly from the moon face. The lunar sphere was brilliant, as though newly washed. Its beams shone on the departing truck. The van of a body was remindful of a shoe box on spools.

From the corrugated shack came Doc Savage's powerful voice. The tones of his men answered.

Buttons Zortell and Jud could not understand the words. But they managed to identify tones.

"All six voices have spoken!" Buttons chuckled. "That means they're all in the dump!"

The voices to which they listened ceased to speak. Lights in the structure went out.

"They can't leave in the moonlight without us seein' 'em!" said Jud. "Moreover, now that the moon is out, there ain't no need of me crawlin' to that barrel an' markin' it with phosphorus. We can see it without that!"

Buttons agreed the mission—it was the one over which they had held the tricky coin match—was now unnecessary.

Both men carefully unwrapped oil cloth from the breech mechanisms of their rifles. This cloth had protected the weapons against the heavy torrential rain.

Together, they drew a bead upon the dimly visible barrel which they had planted close beside the corrugated shack.

"For Pete's sake, don't miss it!" Buttons snarled.

Their rifles *whanged* together. And they did not miss.

There was a flash—all the world ripened into glaring flame. A titanic fist seemed to knock Buttons and Jud end over end. They brought up agonizingly in a bed of prickly pear.

They could hear fragments of corrugated iron raining about them. Their ears ached from the explosion which had just occurred.

"Blazes!" muttered Buttons. "We came near bein' too close to that barrel of TNT!"

Peering in the direction of the shack, they saw it had been erased from the earth. A sizable hole had been scooped out of the ground. No one in the shack could have remained alive.

"Doc Savage got away from our bomb in New York!" Buttons grinned. "But he didn't get away from *this* one!"

The two men scuttled away from the spot, carrying the rifles with which they had detonated the explosive in the barrel.

The blast had snapped Skullduggery into wakefulness. Many windows had been broken. Dishes had jumped off shelves. A stovepipe or two had fallen.

Curious persons piled out of their quarters and made for the scene of the burst. They shouted excitedly. Yapping dogs added to the excitement.

Buttons and Jud separated.

"I'm headin' straight for the new hang-out!" Buttons declared. "It ain't safe for me to stay here in Skullduggery! Too many people know me!"

Jud, after watching his confederate out of sight, concealed his rifle under a parked truck. He turned up his collar and yanked his cowboy hat low.

Not many residents of Skullduggery knew Jud by sight. He was convinced he would not be recognized. He mingled with the crowd. The comments he heard tickled him.

"If there was anybody in that shack, it'll take hours to get their bodies together!" said a man.

"Worse than that," insisted another. "They won't find 'em a-tall!"

Jud smirked widely at this talk.

Then he saw Richard O'Melia.

THE burly construction man had evidently come from the dam site. He was disheveled. Sometime during the night, he had fallen in soft mud to his hips. He wore no hat, and his hair was mud-stained.

Jud watched O'Melia, a strange expression on his villainous face. He licked his lips as if tasting a pleasant thought. His fingers crawled on the grips of his six-guns.

Once Jud turned, as though to leave the scene. But his steps slowed. He wheeled back, his unpleasant face fixed in determination.

"Dad-blame me!" he chuckled fiercely. "I'll do it! I might as well be lookin' out for myself!"

He skulked through the crowd, one eye cocked on the heavens. A cloud was sailing majestically toward the brilliant moon. Jud timed his procedure with the progress of the cloud.

When moonlight was blotted out, he stepped up to O'Melia.

He thorned a gun snout into the construction man's side. He said nothing. No words were necessary.

O'Melia looked down slowly. There was enough light to reveal Jud's revolver.

"What d'you want?" O'Melia asked in a low, angry voice.

"Plenty of silence!" Jud told him. "One bleat—and you'll be pickin' lead outa yourself! Walk ahead of me! We're gonna have a talk!"

O'Melia began: "You dirty——"

"I ain't kiddin'!" Jud warned.

O'Melia snapped his lips together. He permitted himself to be herded away from the crowd. The gun snout bore steadily into his back.

They entered a cluster of yucca which shut off the dancing flashlights being rushed to the blast scene for use in hunting the bodies.

"Start your talkin'!" gritted O'Melia.

For answer, Jud flicked out his left-hand six-gun. He swung it, grunting with the effort. It clanked above O'Melia's temple. The construction man collapsed. Air rushed out of his lungs in a long, blubbering sigh.

Jud hunkered and felt the man's wrist.

"Ain't dead!" he passed judgment. "Don't make any difference, nohow! I'll finish the job disposin' of his body!"

Chapter XIX

TRUCK DEATH

Jud remained beside O'Melia's senseless form for some time. He was thinking. At length he reached satisfactory conclusions. Straining, lips clenched between his snaggle teeth, he got O'Melia on his shoulders.

The explosion scene had drawn almost every one. Jud avoided notice without much trouble, walking swiftly with his burden.

A truck loomed in front of him. It was the machine under which he had hidden his rifle.

Jud lowered his burden. Then he made sure it was a company truck, and that nothing but warehouses were near. This told him he could steal the vehicle without much trouble.

The machine had a steel dump body, and an apron of steel to protect the driver, in lieu of a cab. It was a regulation muck truck, used in hauling excavated rock to the spoil dumps. Jud was familiar with its operation.

He tossed the senseless form of O'Melia into the seat, then cranked the motor into thundering life. His rifle in the seat beside him, he drove hurriedly away.

The machine slithered greasily on the treacherous winding road that led down to the dam site. Jud kept the gears in second for the braking effect they offered.

He did not continue the whole way to the dam. Some distance from it, he turned left on a little-used spur road. This was hardly passable. He kept his eyes ahead, and fought the wheel.

An inspiring panorama opened before him. He quickly stopped the truck, got out, and advanced a few yards afoot. He now stood on the lip of a great cliff. Directly below was the surface of the new lake.

The rippling vista stretched away until lost in the hazy moonlight. The cloudburst had brought enough water to almost completely cover the wide, long valley which was the ancient lake bed.

When completed, the lake was expected to be much deeper. But it would not be much greater in area.

Jud leaned over the cliff brink, and gave the rough, muddy water below an inspection. The look he bent upon it was almost loving. The depth must be many feet—it was in the nature of a sink hole.

He hurried back to the truck. The tool box yielded a length of stout chain. This was intended for use in aiding stalled machines.

Jud tied one end of the chain around the neck of senseless Richard O'Melia. The other end he secured to an axle of the truck.

No foolishness like tying the man in the cab for Jud! This was simpler, more efficient. The truck would take O'Melia over the brink to his death. The splash as it hit the water probably would not be heard—the storm still roared in the north.

Jud got in the seat, latched the shift in low gear, dragged open the hand throttle, and aimed the speeding truck for the cliff. Then he jumped out.

He landed with springy ease—highly pleased with himself. This might be an elaborate method of murder, but it accomplished two things much to be desired. It got rid of the body; it disposed of an expensive truck which belonged to the hard-pressed Mountain Desert Construction Company. The cliff top was a flint-hard rock; it would not retain the truck tracks.

Jud leaped to the cliff edge to watch the truck disappear. A convulsion of staring unbelief drove the evil delight off his face. For a moment, it seemed he would topple over the dizzy rim, so shocked was he.

There was no body tied to the rear of the truck!

EXCITEMENT made Jud's breath rattle loud in his throat. He ran back to see if O'Melia could have dropped off the chain. There was no sign of the stocky construction man.

Jud snarled at his own perturbation.

"The body must've been hangin' under the truck so I couldn't see it!" he grunted.

He glanced about for his rifle, and realized he had forgotten to take it from the truck.

"A fine goof I'm gettin' to be!" he complained. "It's lucky that rifle can't be traced to me, even if somebody does find it!"

The splash of the truck into the lake had not been loud—in his own excitement, he had hardly been aware of it. Nevertheless, he decided it would be a good idea to quit the vicinity.

The large boulders along the trail assumed to Jud's uneasy eyes the shape of crouching men. He hissed at his uneasiness. Drawing both six-guns, he carried them in his hands. They made him feel more at ease.

He had covered perhaps three score yards when a sharp clatter arose ahead. It might have been a pebble scooting from under the boot of a creeping man. It might have been flung from somewhere.

Shelter lay on but one side of the road—in an array of boulders. Jud sailed into these with a leap only a scared man could manage.

One of the boulders seemed to take on life, to acquire great arms and hands, and a complexion of bronze! The metallic hands trapped Jud. They tightened with a terrible force.

Jud was a strong man, a powerful fighter. He had once boxed professionally, as witness his broken nose and cauliflower cars. He had never encountered a man he did not secretly think he could whip, either by fair means or foul. Jud had a great store of underhanded fighting tricks. But he was helpless now.

Through his teeth split such a gurgling scream of agony as the arid Arizona hills had not before heard. His six-guns were milked from his hands and tossed away.

Jud had once thrashed a very small and weak boy for accidentally bumping into him. He had always remembered what a puny little bundle of flesh the kid had been in his hands.

Jud felt like that boy now. Every move he made was thwarted by arms of steel. He swung awful blows—only to have his fists actually seized in midair and shoved back to his side. And wherever the bronze grip of his Nemesis settled, numb and ghastly pain was left.

That such Herculean strength could belong to any man, Jud was loath to believe. He twisted, fighting weakly. For the first time, he got a look at the features of his captor.

Ghostly fright was now added to his troubles. His pain-blurred brain somehow seized on the idea that his attacker was not mortal. His captor had the features of Doc Savage—a man supposed to be dead!

"Golly!" Jud moaned. "You was blowed up——" Pain made the words stick in his throat.

Doc Savage maintained a grim, spectral silence. He knew this would tend to undermine Jud's nerve.

"We heard you an' your gang talkin' in the shack a minute before we blowed it up!" Jud wailed. "You couldn't have gotten away! We'd have seen you in the moonlight! Still—hell! You're real enough——"

Doc still said nothing, although Jud's puzzlement would not have been hard to dispel.

What had happened was simple. Doc and his men had left the shack in the van which had ostensibly brought baggage. A phonograph record bearing their voices, and a time switch to extinguish the lights, explained their apparent presence afterward.

Doc had planned! And the netting of Jud was one of the fruits of his deep-laid scheme!

JUD, instead of falling a victim to complete terror, began to get hold of himself. His hard, blue lips firmed. His little eyes narrowed.

"How'd you get away?" he demanded.

Doc kept a blank face and propelled the man farther into the boulders. Jud caught sight of a form draped against a rock. He started, swore, and began to sweat.

The form was Richard O'Melia. The man was still unconscious.

Jud knew Doc Savage must have unfastened O'Melia from the chain on the truck axle. He did not see how the job could have been done so silently. It seemed impossible. Then he remembered the strength of the bronze man—a strength so great it was frightful. Muscles such as those could accomplish the impossible.

Doc's hands now glided over Jud's stocky form, seeking certain portions of the nerve system. Jud emitted a shrill bleat. After that, he found a terrible thing had happened to his muscles.

Try as he might, Jud could only squirm feebly! He could not understand what had occurred. His knowledge of human anatomy was limited. He failed to realize Doc had simply paralyzed certain nerve centers with pressure, a feat made easy by Doc's intensive surgical training.

Doc now revived O'Melia.

Able to sit up, O'Melia took his head in both hands and groaned. "How'd I get here?"

Doc told him.

O'Melia listened, breathing heavily from the pain in his bruised head. He glowered at Jud as he heard how the man had plotted to murder him.

Suddenly O'Melia sprang to the spot where Jud's six-guns had dropped. He clutched a weapon, aimed it at Jud.

"I'll fix you for tryin' to kill me!" he bellowed—and pulled the trigger.

The gun spoke a clap of a roar. But the bullet only made a shiny smear on a near-by rock. A small stone, flung with unerring accuracy by Doc's hand, not only caused the slug to go wide, but knocked the revolver spinning.

O'Melia clutched his stinging fingers and roared in a wild rage.

"Nobody is gonna try to croak me an' get away with it!" he yelled.

Jud now came to life. He was still unable to move his arms and legs, but there was nothing wrong with his voice.

"Keep 'im off me!" he screamed at Doc Savage. "He's tryin' to kill me to shut my mouth! He's afraid I'll tell!"

"Tell what?" Doc demanded.

Jud bent a snarling glare on O'Melia, who returned it with utter hate. The vicious exchange of looks seemed to decide Jud.

"O'Melia is my boss!" he barked. "O'Melia is the brains back of all this killin' an' construction trouble!"

O'MELIA had all the signs of being stunned by this declaration. Jud went on, his coarse voice lifting to a yell.

"I been gettin' worried!" he bawled. "O'Melia has got stuff on me that'd send me to the pen for life! I was afraid the buzzard would use it! That's why I was gettin' rid of 'im!"

O'Melia now hurtled for the six-gun which had been knocked from his hand. His face was turgid with rage.

But again Doc flung a rock. This one took O'Melia on the head, instead of the hand. The man slumped down amid a rattle of gravel.

"He's my boss!" Jud whined.

Doc said nothing. His fingers sped over Jud's bulky form—and Jud suddenly discovered use of his limbs had returned.

Carrying O'Melia, herding Jud before him, Doc returned to the construction settlement.

O'Melia's private quarters proved to be his destination. A rather substantial bungalow-style shack housed these. There was a bedroom, roughly furnished. The other chamber, a living room, was more elaborately fitted. Indian tomahawks, javelins, knives, Navajo blankets, wampum belts, decorated the walls. Skin rugs of bear, bobcat, and mountain lion were on the floor.

Doc seized Jud, rendered him helpless with nerve pressure, then made a circuit of the bungalow. He was outside several minutes.

Immediately he was back indoors, he returned Jud the use of his limbs. This was an act of kindness, since, under the nerve pressure, the limbs were filled with the unpleasant sensation of being asleep.

A dipperful of water revived O'Melia. A denial of Jud's charge promptly leaped from O'Melia's lips.

"A pack of lies!" he rasped. "The skunk is tryin' to cover his boss, at the same time curryin' your favor by makin' you think he's talkin' freely!"

"Ain't neither!" Jud yelled. "I'm tellin the truth, an you know it!"

"You," Doc told Jud dryly, "wouldn't know the truth if you met it in the road."

"Meanin' you don't believe me?" Jud wailed.

"Exactly. O'Melia stated your motives. You're trying to cover the identity of your leader."

O'Melia gaped incredulously, as if he couldn't believe the good news. An expression of great sheepishness came upon his features. He sat down weakly in a chair, and swabbed his tongue over dry lips.

"Reckon I've made a locoed goat outa myself!" he mumbled. "I've got a plumb cultus temper, and sometimes she gets away from me! Givin' this coyote a killin' was all I could think of, after he sprang his pack of lies!"

Doc Savage replied nothing—he seemed to be concentrating on the use of some one of his faculties. Perhaps his hearing!

Jud whipped to his feet. He had decided to try a break. Head-first, he pitched at a window. Glass jangled; wooden cross-pieces of the sash splintered. Jud vanished into the outer night.

There was a floundering and crashing outside the window. Then feet ran rapidly away.

Doc Savage appeared like a bronze-hued gush of smoke in the doorway. He saw the running figure—a man, doubled low, features obscured by snapped-down hat and the darkness.

The runner whirled and lifted a gun. The weapon spat flame, and a stutter of powder noise. Snapping bullets drove Doc to shelter.

"Hey!" O'Melia wailed. "Where'd Jud get a gun so quick?"

Doc clipped: "Look out of the window Jud jumped through!"

Puzzled, O'Melia complied.

Jud lay on the hard earth under the opening. A long knife had been inserted expertly into his heart.

Chapter XX

THE FIERY TRAIL

THE truth did not dawn upon O'Melia for some seconds.

"The guy runnin' away isn't Jud!" he gulped. "Who is he?"

Doc, instead of answering, exposed himself at the door for a flash moment. A salvo of bullets arrived almost as he whipped back out of view. They tore wood off the door jamb. One smashed the stone head of a tomahawk on the wall; another caused two spears to fall clattering to the floor.

The gunman plunged through a mesquite clump, and could be seen beyond it, dodging around ramshackle buildings until his figure was lost in the moonlight.

"Who was it?" O'Melia repeated.

"My guess is that it was Jud's boss—the devil behind this mess!" Doc replied.

"But why'd he scrag Jud?"

"Two reasons, probably. First, he was afraid Jud could be made to talk. But the fact that he slew Jud, instead of helping him to escape, indicates he wanted his hireling out of the way. Jud had dangerous knowledge, and he was clever enough to use it to his own gain, in the future."

O'Melia studied Doc curiously. He was remembering Doc's air of concentration a moment before Jud made his ill-fated break. Doc had been listening to something——

"You knew some one was prowlin' outside, didn't you?" O'Melia queried of Doc.

"Oh, yes," Doc assured him calmly. "The fellow sought to enter the bedroom window, but failed. Then he came around the house. My intention was to let him reach the window of this room, where he could have been seized. But Jud's act spoiled my plan."

O'Melia's expression was amazed. The bronze man's powers were uncanny, he reflected. O'Melia had heard nothing to indicate a skulker, yet Doc had heard a great deal.

"Aren't you gonna follow the killer?"

"In good time," Doc replied. "It is best the man think he is not trailed. In that case, he might lead us to Miss Aster."

O'Melia thought of something. "Where are your five friends?"

"Buttons Zortell was with Jud when the charge of TNT was exploded alongside our quarters," Doc explained. "My gang is trailing Buttons—hoping he'll give them a line on Lea Aster's whereabouts."

O'Melia laughed, then winced as his head throbbed. He felt a greater confidence in this bronze giant than at any previous time. Until now, he had harbored a vague fear that Doc was not clever enough to cope with the fiend behind all the Mountain Desert's troubles. But O'Melia's doubts had suddenly vanished. Whoever the unknown master mind might be—he had met his match in Doc.

Doc Savage now hurried to his laboratory, transferred from the blown-up shack. He worked over the ultra-violet-light lantern, converting it to battery operation, so that it could be transported easily.

Rejoining O'Melia, Doc showed the construction man something of interest—pools of a viscous fluid outside the bungalow doors, and under each of the windows. Doc had planted these shortly after bringing O'Melia and Jud to the place.

"The prowler walked through this stuff," he explained. "He failed to notice it because the ground is still damp from the rain."

"So what?" O'Melia wanted to know.

Doc focused the ultra-violet lantern on the ground. Footprints instantly appeared, glowing with a faint, uncanny luminance.

"The chemical the fellow walked through!" Doc elaborated. "He will leave tracks for some time, which we can follow by using the lantern device."

Without more delay, they set out on the trail of the fleeing killer.

They did not get far, however. A man appeared, stumbling madly through the moonlight. In one hand he carried a slender blade of steel, red and dripping—a sword cane.

The sword cane was almost a necessity to identify Ham.

He was no longer the dapperly dressed lawyer. His garments were wrecked.

"Buttons Zortell led us into an ambush!" Ham rasped. "Monk, Renny, Long Tom, Johnny—all four were seized!"

NEVER was it more apparent than now that Doc was master over his own emotions. No twinge of feeling altered the metallic set of his features. No catch came into his breathing. Perhaps the flake gold of his strange eyes assumed a slightly molten hue as he heard the bad news. But that was all—no other change.

"The gang has got our four pals?" he said softly, as if to be sure.

"They have!" Ham rapped. "They covered us with guns before we knew what was up. They tied us. I cut myself loose with my sword cane—they didn't know what it was. I tried to help the others, but it was no use! I beat it!"

He snapped red stains off the long, flexible sword cane, and the blade made a song like a hard-stricken harp chord.

"Where did this happen?" Doc questioned.

"In a cactus patch on the edge of town. But the last I saw of the outfit, they were headed for the dam with our pals in tow.

"For the dam!"

"Yes." Ham shook his head, puzzled. "I expected them to light out for the mountains! But they didn't! They seemed to think they would be safe from you, once they reached the dam."

"Did you overhear them say that?"

"Sure."

Doc now took two or three steps backward—and a mesquite clump gobbled him.

"Hey!" gulped Ham, and sprang forward. He did not want to be left out of the fight ahead.

But Doc had vanished—he was even now many yards away and traveling swiftly.

"What'll we do?" O'Melia asked anxiously.

"Twiddle our thumbs!" grunted Ham. "Doc will ring us in when he's ready for us."

"But we can get a posse together and rush the dam!" offered O'Melia.

Ham swung his jaw in an abrupt negative. "Nothing doing! That might spoil Doc's plans, whatever they are!"

The storm still grumbled softly in the distance. The lightning had died away, however, except for an occasional feeble wink. Overhead, a thin and scattered after-storm scud frequently smudged the face of the moon.

The stiff, palmlike shadow of a yucca seemed to give birth to Doc's bronze form. He glided through the moonlight. Under his arm was the boxshaped ultra-violet lantern. It sprayed invisible beams at the ground from time to time, disclosing footprints which glowed with an unearthly quality.

Doc was trailing the slayer of Jud! The fluorescent footprints led in the direction of the dam.

Men appeared ahead. They were workmen from the dam, excited, a bit frightened. Some nursed bruised heads.

Haunting the shelter of sagebrush and mesquite, Doc heard enough of their animated talk to learn what had happened.

A gang of men—between twelve and sixteen in number—had appeared at the dam. Flourishing guns, they had driven off every one but themselves. The workmen, unarmed, not receiving pay as fighting men, had done the sensible thing and departed without resistance.

"The gang had four of Doc Savage's men as prisoners!" said one laborer.

Doc did not make his presence known, but continued on for the dam site. His going was as furtively silent as the stalk of a jungle hunter. And there had come into his manner something of the fierceness of the wild. His enemies would be wise to look to their safety.

QUIET gripped the great dam—the quiet that presaged violence. The gunmen were keeping out of sight. Not a shot had been fired in routing the workmen. But they did not know at what moment hostilities might open.

Uneasiness gripped the gang. They swapped weasel glances and muttered under their breaths. They were wondering what had become of their leader. The fellow had eased himself away from the group.

Had they known the master mind was now out on the dam structure itself, they would have been surprised. Had they known what he was doing, they would have been stricken with terror.

The chief villain was swathed in his gabardine coat. A bandanna and a cowboy hat completed an effective disguise. The man sat under one of the canvas covers which had been spread over the new concrete. He was conducting some interesting experiments.

Between his knees was a small wooden box. Attached to this was a twisted pair of insulated wires—a small cable scores of yards long. The man scraped the insulation from the free end of the twisted pair and arranged the copper wires so the tips were a fraction of an inch apart.

The sinister experimenter now produced a flashlight. He pointed this at a glass window in the box and pressed the button. A hot electric spark leaped between the naked tips of the copper wires.

The man's bandanna fluttered with his gusty grunt of satisfaction. The box held a photo-electric cell, spark coil, batteries. When a light shone upon it, a high-voltage charge of current was hurled through the wire.

If the wires were attached to the proper detonator and embedded in an explosive, a single brilliant light would loosen a blast.

The masked man now proceeded to attach a detonator to the copper strands! This he inserted in a great suitcase of high explosive.

The explosive, he lowered down the inside wall of the dam, letting it sink many yards beneath the dirty, muddy water.

The preparations completed, he kneaded his hands gleefully. A bright light, shown in the canyon depths behind the dam, would result in instant destruction of the great edifice.

The schemer, a muffled and melodramatic figure in his disguise, crept along the dam top. He noticed his shoes were leaving muddy stains, so he halted and wiped them clean. In doing this, he discovered a sticky substance.

Growling, he cleaned this off also. If he gave the stuff any thought, if he wondered in the least where it had come from, he never suspected the truth—that it was a viscous fluid Doc Savage had planted around O'Melia's shack. A fluid that had caused him to leave a trail which became uncannily glowing under ultra-violet rays!

THE gang was relieved to see its leader. The wait had rasped somewhat on their nerves.

"What're we hangin' around here for?" snarled Buttons Zortell. "Blazes! We're wastin' good time! Time we could be usin' to make a get-away!"

"Shut up!" grated the masked man. "Don't question my orders!"

"What're we waitin' on, then?" Buttons was too uneasy to be bulldozed easily.

"I have been setting a trap!" smirked the voice behind the bandanna.

"What kind of a trap?"

"One that is perfect! One that could not be better! Your part of it is to decoy Doc Savage down to the canyon bottom, beneath the dam."

A hiss of uneasiness went up at this. "Supposin' Doc

Savage should blow the dam up? We'd drown! We wouldn't stand a chance!"

Their chief—the man who was sometimes known under the assumed name of Nick Clipton—snarled at their reluctance.

"Savage wouldn't destroy the dam!" he rapped. "You birds get down on the canyon floor! Do a little shootin' from there, so Savage will know where you are. That'll draw 'im down!"

"Supposin' it don't?"

"What else do you think could happen?"

"Doc Savage might take that whirly-gig flying contraption of his, an' try to drop bombs on us," Buttons Zortell said wisely.

"You dope! You'll have four of his men an' the girl along, won't you? He ain't gonna drop bombs on them!"

"Yeah," Buttons admitted. "That's right. Now let's get it straight, what we're to do. We just go down in the canyon an' start shootin'! That's all there is to it, huh?"

"Just one thing more!" snapped their visored chief.

Reaching into his clothes, the man produced a candlelike flare. This was the same type as previously used at their cliff-dwelling landing field. It gave an extremely brilliant white light.

"The minute you see Doc Savage on the canyon bed, light this!" the man ordered, and gave the flare to Buttons Zortell.

"What's it for—a signal?" asked Buttons, somewhat confused.

The masked man hesitated the briefest moment, then chuckled. "That's it! Sure! It's a signal!"

"What'll happen after we signal?" Buttons wanted to know.

"I'll take care of that!" the other snarled. "Quit chewin' the fat an' get movin'! C'mon, drag it! The whole kit an kiboodle of you! Hurry things up!"

He was striving to rush them off. He didn't want them asking questions. Who knew but that they might hit upon the grisly truth? It would not be healthy for the mysterious master mind, should his henchmen learn he was planning for them to die along with Doc Savage, should they suspect his cleverly planned explosive charge, placed at a vitally weakened point of the dam to make possible its destruction. The tremendous weight of the water, the freshly poured concrete—all these would serve the villain now.

The light of the flare, to be touched off at sight of the bronze man, would be brilliant enough to actuate the photoelectric cell. The dam would be destroyed! Not only would Doc perish, but also the villainous gang and their prisoners.

The king killer was going to do more than rid himself of his chiefest enemies! He was going to annihilate all who knew his identity! It was a supreme stroke of wickedness, this thing he planned.

Chapter XXI
ROBOT MEN

BUTTONS ZORTELL led the gang downward through a spillway tunnel. This had been cut in the solid stone canyon walls. It was about fifty feet in diameter. It slanted downward, but not so steeply but that it could be negotiated afoot.

Buttons chose the tunnel because there was less danger, should shooting start. They had four submachine guns, as well as rifles and revolvers. Any one who tried to attack them from the top of the tunnel would have hard going.

No enemies were below on the canyon bed. Some of the gang were in a power house, guarding the prisoners—four of Doc's men and Lea Aster. Men could hardly descend to the canyon depths without attracting their attention.

It was very dark in the vast spillway tunnel.

"Get a move on, you rannies!" snapped Buttons. "I don't know what the boss has got in his sleeve, but it's up to us to help 'im put it over!"

Loose rock, not yet mucked out of the cavernous excavation, clattered underfoot. Echoes rumbled off sides and ceiling.

"I ain't so hot about this!" complained one of the crew. "Supposin' that dam would bust? There's a lot of water behind it! The stuff would come down the canyon like a bat out of hell!"

"Pipe down!" Buttons growled, little knowing the words were in the nature of a finishing touch to his death warrant. "We'll get the prisoners outa the power house the first thing!"

A grayish smear ahead denoted the exit into the gloomy canyon bed.

At this point, there sounded a sudden thump, a flurry of gravel. It was impossible to tell what had happened in the muggy black of the spillway tunnel, since the men were not using lights which might draw bullets.

"What is it?" somebody snapped.

"Dang the luck!" snarled Buttons's voice. "I fell down!"

The others advanced from the tunnel and stood on the

canyon bed. They could hardly see each other in the dark murk.

Buttons Zortell did not appear.

"What's the trouble, Buttons?" a man called.

"I'm takin' a rock out of my shoe!" rumbled Buttons's tone within the tunnel. "You rannies go on to the power house an' get the prisoners!"

The men moved off, complying with this order.

A moment later, a figure scuttled out of the tunnel. The garments this person wore were those of Buttons Zortell, but the movements were extremely unlike the swaggering shuffle usually affected by Buttons.

The form moved with amazing speed for the power house. The swiftness with which the figure moved would have identified it to an observer. It was Doc Savage. He had listened to the men receive their orders—and before that, he had watched the master killer's sinister preparations!

Doc lost no time. He had overpowered Buttons Zortell in the tunnel with such quiet and dispatch that none had suspected. His remarkable command of the art of voice mimicry had furthered the deception. But his work was far from done.

Circling, he evaded the slow-moving gunmen. His superior speed enabled him to reach the great power house in advance of the gang.

A guard stood before the door. He sighted Doc.

"Who's that?" he growled as Doc came closer.

"Who d'you think, you dope!" Doc's imitation sounded wondrously like Buttons Zortell.

The lookout was fooled. He let Doc come within reach—probably because Doc wore Buttons's cowboy hat and jumper.

Cr-a-c-k! To his dying day, the guard carried an impression somebody had hit him on the jaw with a stick of dynamite.

Doc tangled his right hand in the fellow's coat. It was the same right hand with which he had struck the blow. He shoved the unconscious man into the power house.

Two more guards started in surprise. Their hands dived for six-guns. The weapons hung low in tied-down holsters. Their hands did not have far to travel. No doubt they did not dream but that they both could slam lead into Doc Savage before he reached them.

They dropped before they had time to change their ideas. Doc, charging them, was a tawny flash. One man got a poke that set his jaw awry. The second fell after Doc had apparently done nothing more violent than snap a finger against his temple.

It was not often that Doc used his fists. When he did, no blows were wasted. Should he have had to strike a second time, he would probably have added a half hour to his daily exercise routine.

He glided on into an inner room of the power house.

Blonde Lea Aster, her prettiness lessened no whit by her captivity, lay on the floor, bound and gagged. It was obvious she had not been harmed seriously by her captors.

Monk sprawled near by, also roped and silenced. He had been through a fight—his homely face would bear a new crop of scars, for it looked as if somebody had walked on his features with hobnail boots.

Renny and Long Tom had been working on each other's bonds. Johnny had broken the thick magnifying lens of his glasses and was industriously seeking to cut through his own ropes.

They greeted Doc with fishlike flops—the only way they could express their delight.

"QUIET!" Doc's wispy, but penetrant whisper warned.

A knife appeared in his bronze hand. He quickly cut the prisoners free from their bonds.

Then he flashed to each of the group, handing out tiny articles which he took from a padded metal pocket case.

These objects were weird fighting weapons—weapons perfected by Doc Savage and used by no one else. They were metallic thimbles. Each held a tiny hypodermic needle containing a drug which induced a weird helplessness—the victim could see and hear what went on about him, but could not think for himself. He could move, yet being unable to think for himself, never stirred until told to.

Ordinarily, Doc loaded his thimbles with a drug which merely produced instant unconsciousness. But now he was using his more mysterious concoction.

Armed with the thimbles, Doc and his men took up positions outside the power house. Even pretty Lea Aster crouched back of a caterpillar tractor and scrutinized the heavy darkness for quarry.

The gunmen stumbled up, making considerable noise.

They were quickly vanquished. A single concerted swoop by Doc and his aides—their hands stabbed like serpent heads —and their enemies simply stopped in their tracks. Not a shot was fired.

"Drop your guns!" Doc commanded in a powerful voice. Such were the weird effects of the drug that the thugs obeyed. Their thinking processes were paralyzed. They would do nothing unless ordered. For they could not recall Doc was their enemy!

"The way this stuff works always tickles me!" Monk chuckled. "You can take the meanest guy an' it turns him into nothin' but a flesh and blood machine!"

"What are we going to do with them?" Renny demanded.

"The usual thing!" Doc replied.

The others knew what he meant—the institution he maintained in up-State New York, where criminals were made over into honest men by the fantastic brain operations and a course of schooling. These culprits would be sent there!

"Buttons Zortell ain't entitled to that much, even!" Monk grumbled. "He's a murderin', no-good louse! He killed Bandy Stevens."

Doc did not reply. To the drugged prisoners, he said: "Get moving!"

The men moved as through in trances. They might have been unthinking robots. When one bumped into a large boulder, he stood pressing against it, unable to reason that he could avoid the obstacle by going around it! He had to be told what to do!

Doc's men carried the three who had been knocked unconscious. They entered the steeply sloping spillway tunnel. They found Buttons Zortell, lying where Doc had dropped him with a terrific fist blow.

Monk scooped Buttons up.

"This is one guy I sure hate to see escape payment for his crimes!" Monk grumbled.

"WHO's the brains behind all this?" Renny demanded. "Believe it or not, we haven't been able to find out!"

"You shall see before long!" Doc replied grimly.

"Then you know who it is?"

"A suspicion, only," Doc replied gravely. "This man is so diabolically clever that he has managed to cover his footsteps. I have discovered the purpose behind his crimes, however. I have learned the thing he is after."

"What is it?" came the eager chorus.

"You recall the molten rock in the cliff dwelling, and the strange odor which was present?" Doc questioned of them.

"I'll never forget that smell!" Monk grunted. "It was something entirely new!"

"Exactly," Doc told him. "The scent marked the presence of an entirely new gas. A gas previously unknown! A gas which, when burned, produces a heat as great as that of the hottest electric furnace!"

"How'd you find that out?"

"By analyzing the cliff-dwelling air, some of which you'll recall I trapped in a flask. A quantity of this gas was undoubtedly burned in the cliff ruin. It turned the solid rock into lava, blocking the secret passage! Some of the stuff escaped without burning, and it was this which I secured for chemical analysis."

"Holy cow!" Renny muttered. "Where did the stuff come from?"

"That puzzled me for a time," Doc said softly. "But when the master mind went to such pains to get the lake bed flooded, the answer was plain."

"It's under the lake bed, then!"

"Exactly. There must be a vast deposit, since many thousands of dollars were spent in the criminal effort to secure it. The gas, of course, is extremely valuable because of its heat-producing nature. It can be used in welding, smelting —wherever tremendous heat is necessary."

Doc dropped his voice somewhat, for they were advancing up the spillway tunnel.

"The gas was found during test-drilling to learn the water-holding qualities of the lake bed, of course," he went on. "The man who found it set out systematically to break the Mountain Desert concern, so that he might buy the lake bed cheaply. Like all criminals, he was too greedy to share the profits of his discovery with others."

Doc now halted the procession. Some moments, he was silent, as though engrossed in thought.

"We have a task to perform, brothers," he said in a tone which, although low and soft, was absolutely emotionless. "It's not a pleasant task, but the cause of justice demands that we do it."

His men gathered close, lending intent ears. They knew what was coming. Doc was going to hand the master killer his just deserts!

Chapter XXII

THE DEATH LIGHT

THE king killer was uneasy. He crouched in the gloom beside a tool shed. His cowboy hat was hauled low; his gabardine coat draped about him like a toga. He was perspiring and grinding his teeth.

The dam was only a few rods distant.

More than half an hour had passed since Buttons Zortell's departure. Nothing had happened. The chief had ordered shooting down in the chasm beneath the great dam. Yet none had started! He had expected Doc Savage to appear in the vicinity. There had been no sign of the bronze man.

The only occurrence had been a bit of movement the masked man had thought he observed out on the dam, near the center. He had watched, only to discern nothing more. He had dismissed it as the breeze blowing a tarpaulin.

Why didn't something happen? The man was anxious that his photo-electric death trap be sprung. Everything would be settled by that! His enemies eliminated! His gang wiped out so that none could demand a share in his illgotten gains! The Mountain Desert Construction Company would be bankrupt by the loss of their dam! A perfect master stroke!

The man stood up. He had decided he would look around and see why nothing had occurred. If necessary, he would give Doc Savage a tip which would send him into the chasm.

The man turned. His hair raised under his hat. A stifled croak came through his bandanna mask.

Doc Savage stood before him. And there was a terrible light in the bronze man's golden eyes.

The masked man whipped out a six-gun. But a bronze hand struck with the dazzling speed and force of a lightning flash. The gun was knocked far away.

Terror-stricken, the masked man spun and fled. The most convenient route lay across the top of the partially completed dam. He went that way.

An unexpected event now occurred. Out of the great maw of the spillway tunnel popped another running man—Buttons Zortell. He, too, chose the handiest avenue of flight—the dam top.

The two men—master and hireling—bounded onto the dam almost together. They ran wildly for the opposite side of the dam.

Looking back, they were amazed and relieved to see their bronze Nemesis was not overhauling them. In fact, he was not yet upon the dam.

Then the masked man saw a six-gun. It lay on the dam top, in plain view.

The fellow did not stop to reason how the weapon had come there. He saw it only as a means of murder, a tool delivered to him out of a cloudy night sky, that he might slay the giant bronze man whom he feared beyond all beings.

Scooping the gun up, the king killer whirled. He took a deliberate aim at Doc Savage and pulled trigger.

Came a slamming roar! But no bullet left the gun muzzle. Instead, there leaped forth a dazzling white flame sheet. The six-gun barrel had been tamped with photographic flashlight powder!

The masked man screamed. He dashed a hand at his blinded eyes. His mask was shoved off.

He knew his cold-blooded attempt to kill Doc Savage had brought his own death! The flash had actuated the photo-electric bomb! He launched a scream of terror. He was afraid of death.

Another sheet of flame, a thousand times greater than the puff of flashlight powder, crawled up out of the water in front of the dam. Its blaze lighted briefly the face of the master schemer.

It was Nate Raff!

A FLOOD of muddy water boiled up and up and seemed to upset the vast dam structure.

Nate Raff and Buttons Zortell vanished—sank into a howling, foaming, grinding torrent of muddy water, concrete and steel. The canyon walls quivered from the awful shock of the great dam turning over and tearing to pieces. Boulders as large as cars were jarred off the cliffs.

Spray was driven upward hundreds of feet on the chasm sides. The avalanche hit the power houses and they seemed to melt. The whole lake took on a crawling life and sped for the mouth of Red Skull canyon.

Safe on the chasm sides, Doc Savage and his men watched. No word was spoken of the flash-powder-loaded gun which Doc had placed upon the dam—the gun which had delivered backfire justice!

"So it was Nate Raff!" Renny said wonderingly. "But, Doc, he was kidnaped from the plane——"

"No doubt he lied to us about that," Doc pointed out. "The fact that eleven passengers took off in the plane, and eleven burned bodies were found, was my first tip-off to watch the man, Nate Raff."

"But he was a passenger on the plane!"

"If the truth is ever known, we'll probably find Raff hired a man to fly in his place—and himself arranged the destruction of the plane. I think Raff faked his own death so as to be clear of suspicion. No one suspects a dead man. He could have hired agents to buy the lake bed from the bankrupt Mountain Desert concern, and sell the gas rights for a lump sum. He would not have had to appear in the transaction. You recall he had established himself under a fake name—Nick Clipton."

Ham now arrived. He had the surviving Mountain Desert partners in tow. Ossip Keller and Richard O'Melia took a single look at the moaning, squirming flood where their expensive dam had been. And both seemed ready to faint!

At a word from Doc, pretty Lea Aster began explaining to the pair that they were not ruined men—not with a great deposit of very valuable gas at hand. Doc thought slyly that they might enjoy receiving the news from the entrancing blonde.

Renny, Long Tom, and Johnny were guarding the captives. These latter worthies would soon be *en route* to Doc's up-State New York establishment. They would be made into honest men whether they wished it or not.

Over where Lea Aster was talking to a suddenly delighted Ossip Keller and Richard O'Melia, a single word arose above the rest of what was being said. The word was "reward"!

They were talking of Doc's remuneration, of course—money which Doc would turn over to hospitals and charity, as was his custom.

Monk was peering down into the roaring flood in Red Skull canyon. He greeted Doc with a look of lamblike innocence.

"Quite a show, huh?" he grinned, indicating the flood.

"Monk," Doc said dryly. "Weren't you guarding Buttons Zortell?"

Monk assumed an injured expression and indicated his left eye, which was slightly peeled.

"Aw-w, can I help it if he popped me in the glim and got away?" he complained.

Doc kept his face straight. He remembered that Monk had expressed an opinion that Buttons Zortell—murderer that he was—should be meted the fullest punishment. That Buttons should escape from Monk at all was remarkable. That he should escape at just the right moment to meet death on the dam was even more remarkable.

"So he hit you in the eye, eh?" Doc inquired.

"Yeah—that is, I think it was in the eye!" Monk was suddenly wondering if Doc had seen him bump the orb in question on an outcrop of rock in the spillway tunnel!